The Harlin Saga

The Harlin Saga

Part One: Sara's Legacy

Larry Trapp

Xulon Elite

Xulon Press Elite
2301 Lucien Way #415
Maitland, FL 32751
407.339.4217
www.xulonpress.com

Paperback ISBN-13: 978-1-66285-800-0
Ebook ISBN-13: 978-1-66285-801-7

Dedication

Sara's Legacy is dedicated to my beautiful wife of nearly 46 years, Merryl. She has been an inspiration to me and has constantly put my needs ahead of hers at many, many different times. When I was dissatisfied working as a custodian in a public school, it was Merryl who encouraged and supported my decision to return to college to earn my bachelor's degree. She was also instrumental in my ability to earn my master's degree in education.

Beyond that, without Merryl there would have been no Sara Harlin. Merryl's faith and strength were my inspiration when I was creating the character of Sara. No, Merryl did not have the parents that Sara did; she did not go off to another city to find an orphaned boy to raise, and Merryl never worked in a mercantile store nor a mine in Alaska. But she did give birth to the strength of character that you will find in the main protagonist in this story.

Thank you, Merryl. I love you very much.

Acknowledgements

I would like to thank the following people whose help was immensely important to the completion of this book:

Adam Burns (of americanrails.com) for providing information on the V&T Railroad out of Reno, Nevada to Carson City, Nevada and for providing historical time schedules for those trains.

Carol Coleman (of the Nevada Historical Society) for providing information concerning the type of structural building materials used in Reno, NV in 1895, and for giving me information about disastrous fires in both 1873 and 1879.

Sarah Patton (Archivist of the Nevada Historical Society) for providing vital information about boarding houses in Virginia City, NV in the late 19th century, particularly for women and single mothers with children.

Contents

Prelude

Soaring silently through the crisp, early autumn morning air, the bald eagle scanned the land below for any movement that might help satisfy the hunger which was fast approaching. The inevitable onset of the fast-approaching winter would make the quest for food harder and harder. After leaving the sandy, tree-lined shore of the western edge of Lake Michigan, the raptor scanned across the landscape, searching as far as its eyes could to spy the movement of something that would satisfy its hunger. On and on it flew, in a southwesterly direction, seeking suitable prey. It certainly would not take long before the eagle found the treasure that it sought.

As the winged hunter spotted the moving object far below, its piercing cry shattered the silence of the eastern Illinois sky. Far below, the creature was moving quickly down the dusty, narrow road, as if it were desperately making its way to some predetermined and yet unknown destination. In an instant, the eagle accelerated as it descended towards its quarry. And, just as suddenly, the bird saw that its intended prey was beyond its capability to conquer, and again, just as quickly aborted its attack, flying off to seek more appropriate prey.

Chapter One

A lone figure could be seen making her way down the small wagon road that would eventually find its way to the eastern outskirts of the small settlement of Bensenville. Sara Harlin was the lone figure who inched along the road towards her family's business. Her silky blonde hair was set in a low coiffed style, which was how many of the other young adolescent girls wore their hair. She sported a blue and white gingham dress; the blue was just the right color to make the nearly same tint of her eyes almost a deep lavender. As she quickly but pensively made her way along, she was able to drown out the sound of the eagle flying overhead. Sara was deep in thought and her mind was 50 miles eastward to the city of Chicago. Just a short four months ago, the Columbian Exposition had begun. The Exposition was really a world's fair that was meant to showcase the achievement of countries around the world. In honor of the 500-year anniversary of Columbus's discovery of the New World, the fair was affectionately known as the "Columbian Exposition." Now, in the first week of September, it was quickly coming to its completion, scheduled to take place in the last few days of October. Sara had been looking forward all summer for father, mother, and herself to make the trip to Chicago to attend the Exposition.

At least that's what her father and mother, Isaac and Anna Harlin, had promised Sara. It would have been such an easy thing to do, what with Sara's 19-year-old brother Bill to mind the store while rest of the family went off to Chicago. Bill would have been more than happy to stay behind; he really had no desire to participate or see anything the Exposition had to offer. But promises seemed to make no difference to Mr. Harlin. They were something that was always easy for her parents to make, yet there was always some reason, real or fabricated, that made those promises easy to break. Harlin and his wife had both dangled the reward of a week at Chicago's Columbian Exposition before their 16-year-old daughter, Sara. Time and time again her mother and father promised, bribed, and cajoled their daughter only to snuff out the reward as one would blow out a well-lit candle.

Sara had spent the summer dreaming about all the excitement of the Exposition. Each week she wondered if the next week would be the time for them to take the train into Chicago to enjoy a vacation there. What she would give to see the life-sized replication of Columbus's three ships, an actual moving sidewalk of all things, and, of course, Buffalo Bill's Wild West Show!

Besides these marvels of science that Sara read about in the weekly newspaper, there were also many amusements being showcased. Everything she read about stirred her imagination and filled her mind with awe. Sara wanted more than anything to experience the 'new-fangled' ride they called the Ferris Wheel. She was curious to know how anything in the world could hold 40 people and take all of them more than 260 feet in the air.

Although she had missed this "event of the century," Sara was bound and determined to experience as much as she could at the

Columbian Exposition. She would get there if she had to steal away at night and walk all the way.

All these thoughts flowed through her mind as Sara made her way as quickly as she could to the Harlin Dairy and Farm Supply Emporium. She was once again late and knew that her mother would be standing there in the warehouse-like floor room ready to ask a wide array of questions about why she was so late. Of course, her father would have probably already developed his own theory to explain Sara's tardiness, and there was really no reason to even try to explain anything.

As Sara finally made the last turn down the access road, she saw the Emporium standing about 500 feet ahead of her. The Emporium, as it was affectionately called by the old-timers in town, was owned and operated by the Harlin family.

Nearly 20 years previously, the settlement of Tioga, as it was called then, grew right along with the Milwaukee Road railway. Sometime around 1873, a post office was established and the name of the community was changed to Bensenville, in honor of the German city of Benzen. While the railroad had made the growth of the town possible, it was still the local farms and dairies that gave the railroad reason to be there. For this reason, the newlywed couple, Isaac and Anna Harlin, migrated from the relatively new state of West Virginia about eight years after the Civil War to open their supply store along what would become Center Street. The Emporium continued to grow and thrive as the farmers and dairymen flocked there to purchase their needed supplies. Now, seven years before the turn of the century, the nation found itself in the throes of a severe depression. But people are always going to need food and milk, and farmers are going to need to purchase the tools they needed to provide those staples. Because of the loyalty of their customers, the Harlin family was able to weather the storms of these desperate times. Mr. and Mrs. Harlin would more than likely rationalize their failure in taking Sara to the Columbian Exposition with what seemed to them a reasonable answer: 'who needed Ferris Wheels and Wild West Shows when at least they were able to put food in the ice box, and shoes on their feet?'

Slipping past the idle railroad cars in the train yards just east of the town proper, Sara made her way towards her family's store. Lying just at the edge of Bensenville, there was nothing in particular about the establishment that could be described in endearing terms. It looked just like what it was supposed to look like. After all, how frilly can anyone make a farm supply store? Outside the main store proper, a few wagons were lined up next to a harvesting machine that was being sold for a "Great Price"—at least that's what the sign posted to the harvester stated. Against the 6,500 square foot building that looked more like a warehouse than anything else, were several yet-to-be-opened crates and cans, each containing different accoutrements that were necessities for dairy and truck farmers.

Sara quietly entered through the service door of the Emporium, trying to remain hidden from the glancing eyes of customers in the store, and especially her father, who she was sure would want to delve into the reasons for Sara's late appearance. Sara did not want to deal with the probing questions she knew that both her mother and father would be asking. It seemed that she could never escape the continuous quarries about her day and her moods. If she could slip quietly through the back door, she would be able to go directly to work and maybe – just maybe – she could be left to her own thoughts.

But this was not to be. The hinges of the back door desperately needed oiling, and the screeching noise emitted by the door rivaled the eagle she had heard earlier on her solitary walk to the

Emporium. The opening of the door announced Sara's arrival, which was accompanied with several heads rotating toward the source of the offending sound. Among the barrels and boxes of supplies befitting any farm supply store were a throng of shoppers, each one seemingly annoyed by what they deemed an intrusion. Seeing that the newcomer was just Isaac's daughter they quickly turned back to their business at hand.

Sara saw her brother trying to convince an inquisitive dairyman of the advantages of purchasing the new Thistle steam-powered vacuum milking machine. It was more than apparent that try as hard as he could, Bill was not going to be able to convince the dairyman, and all the effort being put forth was going to be fruitless.

Anna also knew that her time could be more well-spent in some other endeavor. Staying there to be involved with this transaction that was never to occur would be a fool's errand. Quietly, she left Bill to deal with the reluctant customer while she went to deal with her daughter, Sara.

"Well, girl! It's about time you be showin' up. You might consider gettin' to work around here."

"Sorry, Ma. What needs doin'?"

"Girl, you been workin' this store practically all your life and still don't know that work here never gets done. Why don't you go through that crate of seeds put the stock into the bins?"

As Sara started making her way towards the unopened crates and boxes lined up against the back wall, she noticed that her father was not anywhere to be seen. It would be awfully nice if he would just be around once in a while to help the rest of the family take care of business. But it seemed that he was always preoccupied with other business—and that business usually had nothing to do with the store or the family. It seemed that Isaac Harlin was becoming more and more engaged with politics around town and less and less engaged with his store or his wife and kids.

And just as that Sara was starting to open the crates containing the seed orders Harlin appeared through the front door of the Emporium. He was almost a double of his son, Bill. Isaac, or Mr. Harlin, as he preferred that everyone else in town refer to him, was visibly distressed. With piercing blue eyes and thinning grayish blonde hair that sported a bushy "mutt-in-chop" crop on the side of his head, Isaac scanned the occupants for the presence of his wife. It was obvious that he had something to talk about and he wanted to talk about it now. As he finally saw Anna, and caught her attention, he motioned with a curt nod of his head for her to meet him in the office.

No sooner had the two entered the room and closed the door behind them, did Isaac begin his rant. "Anna, you will not believe what they're doin' now!"

"Whose doin', Isaac?"

Collapsing in the chair behind his desk, Harlin continued, "Anna, you know very well that I've been down to the Party Hall talking to the boys. You will not believe the latest rumors goin' around!"

"I know you're bound to tell me, Isaac."

"Darn right I am! You know how the Exposition hired all of those Irishmen, and whatever else kind of foreigners to work over there in Chicago at that event?"

"Yeah, I guess I rightly do."

"Well, it seems that since the things are gradually closing down now, all of those outsiders have decided to head out through the country to look for work. Imagine, Anna, we are lookin' at the possibility of hundreds and hundreds of Micks, Herms, Polacks moving into our little town here; and not to mention those porch monkeys from down south."

"Are you sure it's that bad, Isaac?"

With not a little exasperation, Isaac answered, "That bad! Anna, it's worse than that! You know the Fergusons. You know; the ones who live just down from us?"

"Sure, Isaac, I know Jim and Nora Ferguson very well. Jim was in here just last week to purchase some tools to work over his plow. I believe he bought a plow sharpening tool."

"Well, it seems that his new hire, some Russki or something by the name of Polchev, will be using that new tool."

Somewhat amazed, Anna answered, "I don't recall Jim saying anything about having someone new working for him."

"I would suppose not. Anna, you know where the Party stands and how we feel about this. You know that we Nativists have made some fantastic strides in trying to protect ourselves from this very thing."

"I know that I've been hearing about a new group called the Immigration Restriction League forming up over in Boston. I even hear that there might be a branch in Chicago."

Isaac slid the desk drawer open and pulled out a revolver that had been concealed there. As he held the gun pointed at a map of the county on the wall directly across the room from him, Isaac sighted down the barrel with one eye closed. With a menacing resolve he said, "All I know, Anna, is that none of my family will ever give quarter to those people!"

At that, Harlin rose to his feet, strolled out from behind the desk and slid the gun into the inside pocket of his frockcoat that was hanging from the coat rack near the door. With a curt nod to his wife, Isaac donned the coat, slipped out the back door of his office, and headed north to where he knew other members of the Bensenville Nativist Party normally congregated.

Arriving at Geisler's Billiard Parlor great room, Harlin soon spotted others with whom he was well acquainted. Newel Bender seemed to be dominating the animated conversation which Harlin's friends were having. As he approached the group of men, Harlin could hear Newel seemingly concluding his rant.

"...and by God, that's what I intend to do. If you're in with me, you know where I can be found."

Seeing Harlin, Bender immediately made his way over to talk to him.

"What say, Harlin? Just having a little talk with the boys here."

"I see that. Couldn't help hearing what you just said there. What are you thinking about doin' Newel?"

"Listen, Isaac. I know that the Fergusons are nearly your next-door neighbors, but you and I both know that they went and done something that cannot be tolerated. If we don't take care of this right now, we're going to lose this country."

"So, what is it that you have in mind for the Fergusons?"

"You know as well as I do that we can't abide them aiding and abetting these foreign scumbags they have out there on their farm who, for want of a better word, are sponging off of them."

"I'm with you, Newel. How do you think we should go about this?"

"Okay, so here's what I'm thinking."

In the storeroom of the Emporium, as she continued unpacking the crate of seeds, Sara was in deep thought about a young couple just a few miles away. Out at the Ferguson farm, Janos and Soninka

Polchev were trying their best to survive. The couple had immigrated from somewhere in Eastern Europe not more than a year ago, and Janos was quickly hired to work at the Columbian Exposition until the end of last month. For the past two weeks, Sara had been busy finding out a little bit about the Polchevs. Even though the two struggled with English, they still both worked hard from sunup to sundown, and the Fergusons were extremely delighted in having taken them in. Just in the little amount of time since the Polchevs had arrived in Bensenville, Nora Ferguson was making tremendous headway in getting to know the young couple and teaching them more of what they needed to know to survive in America. Soninka Polchev was especially adept at learning the nuances of all the terminology and oddities of the language and was able to help her young husband Janos understand as much as he might need.

Sara recalled having asked Mrs. Ferguson about the couple and why she had taken in someone like them. It wasn't quite a scolding that she received from Mrs. Ferguson, but she did know somehow that Mrs. Ferguson believed that there was something not quite right about her parents' ideas and beliefs. As Mrs. Ferguson put it, "something not too charitable!"

Sara remembered the conversation she had just yesterday when she tried to defend her mother and father, but somehow, she felt lacking in the level of her parents' convictions. She recalled asking, "Mr. Ferguson, is it right for you to be takin' in 'those kinds of people'?"

"Land sake's, child! What do you mean 'those kinds of people'?"

"You know, Mrs. Ferguson. All those other countries out there; those places over there in Europe. Ma and Pa told me that we might as well start lettin' pigmies and head-hunters into our cities and towns."

Mrs. Ferguson, now in her mid-fifties, had heard a lot of this kind of talk for the past few years. Her husband and she were well aware that the people in this part of the nation were a little bit tired of the intrusions into their lives over the past decade. First, it was the migration of the former slaves from the Confederate South after the Union soldiers had defeated their cause. Former slaves, with no skills other than knowing how to grow, harvest and tend cotton began moving into this part of the country. And now, because of the tremendous amount of unrest and revolution taking place in Europe, more and more people were immigrating from parts of the world that were particularly exotic or unknown to the average person. The things Sara was saying were not new.

"Sara," conjectured Mrs. Ferguson, "are you sure you understand all that you are saying?"

Sara had not really given any of this too much thought. Really, all she was doing was absorbing the sentiments of her parents, especially her father, and then parroting the same things she heard her father say around the house. It was quite natural that she would be repeating all that Mr. and Mrs. Harlin said in her presence. Maybe Mrs. Ferguson knew more about the world and these kinds of things than her father or most of the rest of Bensenville thought she did. At least that was what Sara was beginning to think.

"I'm really not too sure about any of this stuff, Mrs. Ferguson. All I know is what Pa tells us at home."

"Sara, let me try to help you understand a few things so that just maybe you can decide for yourself what's what. I know what those men are saying at the Nativist meetings so I think that maybe we might need to dig a little deeper into what they're really all about. Sara, do you really know what an immigrant is?"

Thinking for just a moment, Sara responded, "Sure, I do, Mrs. Ferguson. Pa has always told us about how our family got to this country from back in the 'Old Country.' I believe it was from somewhere in Scotland."

"Exactly! And what do you suppose your people were when they got here, Sara?"

Suddenly, it became apparent to the young girl that quite possibly she hadn't been seeing things clearly enough.

"Don't you see, Sara? Your ancestors immigrated to this country. Some of them probably had to go through an extremely difficult process just to start from zero in this country. Most likely they had very little money, no family, and not many friends."

"But Mrs. Ferguson. Pa told us that these people coming here from all these other countries are not like us."

"In what way are they not like us Sara? They came through the entry island in New York just like your people did. They went to work making something of themselves, same as anyone else. Sara, you know that Mr. Ferguson and I have taken in a young couple from the eastern part of Austria-Hungary, don't you? I believe they're from somewhere called Bohemia."

"Yes, mam."

"They are the Polchevs; Janos and Soninka Polchev. Sara, I don't know anyone else that has worked as hard as I've been watching that poor Mr. Polchev these past few weeks. Since we took him and his wife in after he was fired from his work at the fair, he has worked constantly around our farm, doing odds and ends that need to get done.

"Mrs. Polchev is doing everything she can fixing up the outbuilding behind our house. She's done all that she can to make what most people around here would call a barn into a comfortable home, and her husband, Janos cares for her so much. He's just about killing himself trying to make a decent life for the two of them. Neither one of them is trying to do anything to hurt this country, and as far as I can see, they're doing everything possible to make it a better, more productive nation."

Getting up from her chair, Nora Ferguson walked over to the book stand in the den and retrieved her Bible. Returning from the stand she said, "Sara, your family goes to church, don't they?"

"Ma'am, we go every chance we get."

"Let me read something to you that Jesus himself said. Here it is in Matthew. Jesus said, 'I was a stranger, and ye took me not in; naked, and ye clothed me not; sick, and in prison, and ye visited me not. Then shall they also answer him, saying, Lord, when saw we thee an hungerd, or athirst, or a stranger, or naked, or sick, or in prison, and did not minister unto thee? Then shall he answer them, saying, Verily I say unto you, inasmuch as ye did it not to one of the least of these, ye did it not to me.'"

"Mrs. Ferguson, are you saying that there something sinful about my family?"

"No child! I'm just saying that we ought to look at the way we treat the less fortunate as a way to serve Christ. We ought not to look at others as anything other than someone who needs ministering to."

Sara was silent for a good while. Mrs. Ferguson had struck a chord with her, and she was beginning to look at things slightly differently from when she began talking to the neighbor.

Nora Ferguson continued, "Sara, just pray about what we've talked about today. This is something that you need to settle with the good Lord."

Now, considering all of this, Sara was beginning to find it harder and harder to be a dutiful Harlin daughter. Sara was realizing that she might be starting to harbor some of the sentiments that Mrs. Ferguson had shared with her. She felt that it could be possible that she was jumping to unwarranted conclusions about people when she really should think differently. It might help if she could get a chance to talk to Soninka Polchev. She knew that Soninka was just a couple of years older than her, so maybe the young immigrant could help her sort some things out.

Two hours later, Sara was able to get away from the store. Once she left, she headed directly toward her home, but Sara intended to make one stop before getting there.

Sara was making very good time as she left the store and town and started heading towards her family's home. The temperature had risen throughout the morning and the humidity was quickly rising. It was not unusual here in this part of the country for the weather to begin cooling down rapidly in the fall, but this would not happen until the end of the month. Now, in the first week of September, the days were warming up to seventies. The thermometer at the shop was climbing up to a pleasant seventy-two degrees, but because of the amount of humidity today the walk along the wagon road was becoming somewhat less bearable. The pace that she set for herself was causing tiny drops of perspiration to bead-up on her forehead. A tall glass of cool water might hit the spot. She hoped that the Soninka Polchev would be hospitable enough to offer something to drink.

The road that Sara followed was not much wider than a single buckboard wagon, and little wisps of a breeze was causing the dust to be stirred up. Each tiny gust of wind created patches of dust clouds she had to endure. Sara was beginning to think that it might have been better had she made the journey to the Ferguson farm walking over the long gentle slope to the east rather than using the roadway.

Finally, spotting the turn-off to the Ferguson farm at the next sweeping curve a couple hundred yards ahead, Sara mentally breathed a sigh of relief. Reaching the turn-off, she gladly departed the roadway and began walking the long wagon drive up to the house. At least the wind driven dust would be a smaller problem to deal with.

About a few hundred yards ahead, Sara could see the small side house behind the barn that served as a cottage for the Polchev couple. It was a tidy looking little home with things seemingly in order. A few goats and a couple of calves were wandering around near the cottage trying their best to find another sweet morsel of wild grass on which to grab a late afternoon bite. Sara was thinking that this was a truly pleasant and cozy sight, as she made her way to the small house.

Sara noted that since the last time she was here, the small out-building had grown more and more to look like a small, tidy, clap-board house rather than just a storage barn like it used to be. There was now a comfortable raised porch that looked inviting to sit on with a cool drink of some kind.

As Sara stepped up onto the porch and crossed over to knock on the door, she could hear the sound of a man, speaking with a strange accent, "Soninka, nemyslím si, že budeme vydělávat dost peněz, pokud zůstaneme…"

"Janos, please. English please. You know we must be Americans now. You must use, please," Soninka reminded her husband.

"Soninka, is ...so ...hard. I try for you. I think we not make too much money if we stay."

"Janos, is best, I think to do as Mrs. Ferguson says, to trust God. He has blessed us great. Is wrong, I think to not trust Him, Janos?"

"Můj miláček ...my darling, I am shamed, but this scares me."

"Yes, yes, it is frightening. It is a hard change for us, but we must believe that God give us our need. It is true we are so far from our family in Pisek, but people in Mr. and Mrs. Ferguson's church give help to us."

"Oh, Soninka! You try to find help where it may not be I think," the young Polchek replied.

"What is it that you say, Janos?"

"I say everything is not what you think. You say these people be our family, but why does family not accept us? Why are we remaining like mouse that looks in, always to be chased by cat in house?"

"Janos, Mr. Ferguson leaves his boots in the tool shed, yes?"

"Ano...I mean 'yes' is right!"

"Boots not tools, yes?"

"Yes, Soninka, you say good."

"So, Janos, is true church people here do not accept us. I think maybe we don't need to be accepted by them. I'm thinking maybe because a cat keeps a mouse out of the house, it might not be a member of the family of that house."

Janos had much to think about. He turned, deep in thought, and began to walk to the door, not knowing that Sara was outside the door quietly eavesdropping on the conversation within the room. Sara heard the sound of Mr. Polchev's boots approaching the door, so she moved as quickly as she could off the porch, hoping her nosiness would not be discovered. But, in her haste to get away, she caught the toe of her shoe on a loose board and tumbled onto the ground.

The moment that Janos opened the door, he saw the prone form of the young girl who was lying face down in a small puddle of mud beyond the porch steps. Sara desperately wanted to sink into the ground, out of sight, but there she lay, with her dress and face covered with a layer of ooze. She wanted to remain face hidden in the mess, but that would require being equipped with gills or some other method of breathing dirty water.

The only reaction Janos made, upon seeing what happened to Sara, was to help her up and only call out to his wife, "Soninka, you must come to help!"

Coming swiftly and deftly out the door, Soninka saw the young girl, sprawled out in the mud, and did all that she could do to keep from bursting out in laughter as she saw Sara sitting in the puddle. Realizing that the girl was not really hurt, other than her pride, all Soninka could manage to ask was, "Are you being okay?"

The next sound made was the pent-up laugh that the young wife was restraining, and even Sara could not hold back as she finally realized how ridiculously funny she must look.

Bundled up in the large quilt that Soninka provided for her, Sara was enjoying the tall glass of lemonade that had been provided for her. Soninka had spared no hospitality as she even included a few pieces of chipped ice in the glass. She assured the young girl that it would not be too many days until the ice man would be delivering another order, so Sara did not feel guilty for partaking in this small pleasure.

The muddy dress had been thoroughly washed and wrung out now and was hanging in the mid-afternoon sun so it could dry. As Soninka came in from checking on the dress hanging on the line behind the house, she reported, "It should not be too long now; dress is drying well."

"Thank you so much, Mrs. Polchev," Sara answered.

"Is nothing. Please, call me Soninka."

"You have been so kind, Mrs. Pol...I mean Soninka."

"Please, is only lemonade for your stomach, soap and water for dress. But what finds you coming to my home, Miss, uh, ..."

"I am so sorry. My name is Sara. Sara Harlin. I guess you could say that I'm a seeker, Soninka. I'm just wanting to find out for myself what I really need to learn. I don't want to know what other people think; I want to know what's true."

"So, Sara, how is I fit search for knowing what is true?"

"Soninka, in the hour or so that I have been here, you have been more than helpful, and you are helping me understand a lot."

Since Sara had been brought in to remove most of the mud and dirt, she had been watching and listening to the young immigrant woman. What she saw was not what everyone had been telling her about people from other countries. The home was well kept and clean, there weren't half-empty alcohol bottles strewn throughout the house, and of all things, Sara saw a Bible lying open on the dining room table.

Sara remembered her conversation with Mrs. Ferguson. She had told her that Soninka was making the best of a desperate situation. The little home she and Janos lived in seemed quite comfortable for the two of them. How could the Polchevs be as vile as most people in this town said they were when she saw that there really was nothing strange at all about them. Sara thought that it might be time to broach a subject that she was a little bit afraid of talking about herself.

"Soninka, do you and your husband have a relationship with Jesus?"

This caused Soninka to stop and slowly turn towards Sara. She quietly moved to the chair next to Sara's and settled into in earnest.

The expression drawn upon her face was one of a mixture of apprehension and at the same time wonder. It was obvious that Soninka was trying her best to compose her thoughts.

"Sara, we find America from small Bohemian town called Pisek. Janos and I both have lived all life as being good Catholics. This idea you ask about having a relationship is something we know nothing about. We ask priest in the church at Pisek for make lives right after, what you say ...our sin, but I'm afraid we be too bad to be good for Christ."

"Soninka, ...I'm sorry. Do you have any idea what your name is in English?"

Sara could see by the scowl on her face that Soninka was trying hard to conjure up the English equivalent to her name. Soon a smile brightened her face as she said, "Yes, yes, is meaning, Sophie."

"May I use that name? It would be so much easier for me, if you don't mind."

"I think is good to do. Please use."

"Thank you, Sophie. Have either Mr. or Mrs. Ferguson talked to you about personal faith in Christ? Have they explained about being 'born again?'

"Yes, I think they try, but is so hard to know."

"To understand?"

"Yes, too hard."

Sara nodded towards the Bible she had seen on the table and said, "Have you read very much in your Bible?"

"Oh, Miss Sara, English is hard for me. I try. Not good to knowing it."

"Please Sophie, just call me Sara. I would like to help you to understand some of your Bible, if you don't mind."

"Oh, Miss ...I mean Sara! Please do for me. I think is best for me to know."

"Oh, Sophie, it is absolutely necessary for you to know. And then I'd like to help you with your English; if that's okay with you."

Sara found herself spending a great deal of time at the Polchev house, teaching her knew friend Soninka, or Sophie, as she insisted that Sara call her. She was also helping Sophie to understand more about the words written in the Bible, especially those in the Book of Romans that explained how everyone was in need of salvation through faith, and faith alone, in Jesus Christ.

Sophie was an eager student, and many times would ask Sara questions about her own faith. When Sara shared from Romans 3:23 that 'all have sinned and come short of the glory of God,' Sophie had to interrupt the discussion.

"Sara, the Bible say 'all sin'?"

"That's right, Sophie. Everyone has sinned. You have, I have, Janos has; it means

that everyone in the world; well, everyone but Jesus Christ."

"Priest in Pisek is a sinner?"

"That's right, Sophie," Sara replied with emphasis. "The priest there, priests here, goodness Sophie, the pope himself even sins just as much as we all do."

The look of horror on Sophie's face was a mixture of shock and denial. "Sara, this is very hard to understand. How can you say Pope Leo is sinned? He is so good!"

"Sophie, that is what Isaiah meant when he wrote that our righteousness is just like filthy rags. The best that we can do is nothing compared to what Christ has done for us."

"Sara, if we are all sinning every day, how do we be saved?"

And now the door was opened. Sara would not waste this opportunity to present the plan of salvation to Sophie. For the next thirty minutes, that is exactly what she did. It was not long before the truth of her need for Christ became fully apparent to Sophie. And, when Sara finally asked her if she wanted to accept the redemption of Christ, she readily accepted Christ as her personal Savior.

The next few weeks a whirlwind of events occurred all around Sara. So much was happening at both the Emporium and at the Polchev home. Her mornings were centered around the events occurring at the shop. Farmers needed supplies to make sure that the harvest this season was successful. Dairy farmers needed to replace equipment that was becoming badly worn. Of course, all the farms and dairies had to be 'wintered'; that is, prepared for the onset of what was always a harsh winter in this part of the country. No one wanted to be negligent in stocking up supplies, as it was not uncommon for occasional blizzards and other forms of inclement conditions to take over the lives of the inhabitants here in DuPage County.

Along with all the work that Sara had to do at the shop, she also had a growing relationship with the Polchevs, and she felt something akin to sisterhood for Soninka. The young woman was doing remarkably well adapting to the language and customs of her adopted country. With Sara's help, she made tremendous strides in that direction. The hours of conversation and laughter that the two young women had shared was priceless. They truly were becoming best friends, and, as Sara was beginning to feel, like long, lost sisters who finally found each other.

Janos's adjustment was a completely different tale. He was finding it harder and harder to be satisfied with what he felt was just handyman work for the Fergusons. He knew that Jim and Nora Ferguson were sacrificing much to provide a living for Janos. As the crops had finally been harvested, it seemed that Mr. Ferguson was finding it challenging to keep Janos busy. The last thing that the young couple wanted was to be a burden on the older couple who seemed more like parents to them than employers.

So, as autumn of 1893 was quickly winding down and the entire community began getting ready for Christmas, a new complication arose for Sara. There are always people in any given situation who delight in spreading vicious rumors and news just to watch chaos and unhappiness unfold. Customers began telling Anna and Isaac that their youngest child had been seen coming from and going to the Ferguson's farm. Harlin and his wife wanted to know who Sara was visiting and why. Of course, with the young immigrant couple residing there at the Ferguson farm, it was a forgone conclusion, at least to Isaac, that Sara was going behind his back to make some kind of accord with the young couple. To Isaac Harlin, this was totally intolerable and must be stopped at all costs.

"Soninka! Are you alright?"

From the retching sound emanating from the Polchev house, Sara could easily tell that something was not quite right. Soninka's face was ashen, and she walked unsteadily to the front door to greet Sara.

"Sophie, I know something's not just right. A person could hear you throwing up all the way up on the county road."

"Oh Sara! This is so true. All morning long I just lose my stomach. Every day since last week, I feel so sick."

Suspecting the obvious, Sara asked, "Sophie, have you had your time ... you know, is your time regular?"

"Sara, I am very late. More than three months have passed."

"That answers a lot of questions, Sophie. Haven't you noticed your dresses getting a little bit tighter, especially in your tummy?"

"Sara, I think you are right. I have felt this way some time, and now I am certain I am with child."

To Sara this was great news. Without a thought, she rushed to Soninka and embraced her in a hug. But the hug that Soninka returned was half-hearted. Sara could feel the tension within her friend and, looking at her, could see the fear and anxiety rising in her.

"Sophie, talk to me. This is one of the greatest ways that God can bless you, but I see you are afraid. What is it?"

Suddenly breaking down, Soninka replied through her tears, "Oh Sara, I am so afraid! This is a time for joy, but for me, it is also a time for worry. It would be good blessing for Janos and me to have baby. But Sara, how can we?"

"What do you mean, Sophie?"

"Janos tries to work so hard. Mr. and Mrs. Ferguson have sacrificed so much for us to be able to live here. They just about let us live here free. But that is just two of us. With baby, things get harder."

Sara saw the truth in what Soninka was saying. It was hard enough for the immigrant couple to get by as just two. Now there would be the child, and she was sure that not many people in this town would ever accept another, so-called, 'one of them.' This was truly going to be something which would require the Lord's intervention. Humanly speaking, things looked desperate for the

Polchevs, but she knew that God was never surprised about anything, and this was all in His plans.

Sara tried to reassure Soninka that things would be fine and that she would be praying for her. She knew that she needed to get home before her father did, but she also did not want to leave her dearest friend. Janos suddenly opened the door, and Sara could see that he wanted to speak to his wife. Giving Soninka a reassuring hug, Sara left.

As Sara was walking down the wagon road that would take her back to the main thoroughfare from Bensenville, she spotted her father's horse-drawn buggy coming quickly towards her. As her father spotted her, he began whipping the horse more forcefully to accelerate the carriage. This was just about as angry as she had ever seen her father, and she was pretty sure she knew why he was so irritated.

As he drew next to his daughter, Isaac pulled hard back on the reins in order to stop the horse. The buggy almost turned over due to the imbalance of the rig, but Harlin was able to keep all four wheels on the ground.

Staring straight ahead, as if refusing to acknowledge her, Isaac said in a coldly menacing voice, "Girl, get in the wagon now. You're done here, do you hear me?"

Sara dutifully ascended into the rig, and without saying another word, Harlin snapped the reins, causing the horse to pull. Without much concern as to whether anyone stayed put in the buggy, Isaac turned it around and headed back towards the main road, and on to his home.

Janos was seated at the small dining room table with is elbows propped up, hands folded with fingers entwined, and pressed up against his mouth and chin. He stared into space, and Soninka knew that many thoughts were coursing their way through is mind. He looked like a person who was on the verge of making a momentous decision, which was, of course, just what he was about to do.

Looking across the table to Soninka, who had sat down there soon after he did, Janos said, "Soninka, miluje tě!"

"Yes, Janos, and I love you, too. Please try in English."

"Soninka, I know!"

"You know? You know what?"

"I know you are in way of being mother. I also know having child now is to be hard."

"What do you say, Janos?"

"I say we struggle now. We try hard, but nothing good happens. Soninka, I must find work situation."

"Oh Janos, no one here gives you work, except Mr. Ferguson."

"I hear of jobs in Chicago open soon."

"Janos, what jobs?"

"Soninka, Mr. Ferguson say, railroad strike coming. Trains need workers. Janos good worker. Can learn to do good job."

"Janos, you would leave farm?"

"I would take care of you Soninka...and new baby to come."

"When will we go, Janos?"

"I think maybe I go so to work. You stay for baby."

"There is just one way you will go, my dear husband. Where you go, I go also."

"This is not easy plan, Soninka. This is hard. Best that you stay."

"My mind is decided. No, you go, and I go. That is it!"

Janos knew that there would be no way he could argue with his wife. She would not stand for them to be separated. If he were to go through with this plan, then he must consider Soninka in his plans. He would need to think about what his next move would be, but he knew that there were no answers here in Bensenville. It would have to be back to Chicago.

Sara sat in the chair that was situated in the middle of the kitchen of her home. She was confronted by both Isaac and Anna Harlin, who circled the poor girl like lions preparing themselves for the final attack to kill their prey. The pressure upon Sara was intense, as her parents both wanted answers, and they wanted answers without any further delay.

Mr. Harlin seemed to take charge of the interrogation as he said, "Now look young lady, your mother and I want answers and we want them now."

"Pa, I've been hearing how you and Ma have been talking about the immigrants coming into our part of the country. I know you think that they are evil, or somehow, they are going to destroy us. I was just trying to find out for myself. I just thought …"

"That's where you're wrong, Sara! You don't think. You just do what you want to do!"

Mrs. Harlin joined in, "Dear, you just need to listen to your parents and obey."

"Ma, I thought you always said it was best to listen to the Lord and obey Him. Besides, I didn't see the Sophie or Janos doing anything that would hurt anyone."

"Listen to the girl, Anna. She's even calling these, ...these people by their first names; as if she wants to be their best friend!"

"Pa, why can't we even call them by their name?" Sara asked.

"Sara, this is what I'm telling you now. I don't care if they have names or not. You are not to visit these people again. Do you understand me?"

"But Pa, Sophie has professed faith in Christ! I've led her to Christ. Doesn't she deserve to be able to be helped in her spiritual growth?"

"What she deserves is to go back to where she came from and learn what she needs to know from her pope. That's what I think, Sara."

Sara did not know what to say. What her father was telling her felt so outrageously wrong, but she also knew that she was in a terrifically difficult situation. Should she not "honor her father or mother" by disobeying them, or should she go behind their backs and help her new sister-in-Christ grow in her new-found faith?

Sara had never been one who would be defiant towards her parents. The very thought of disobeying them was beyond her comfort level. Sara knew that she would be compliant to her parents' wishes, but she also knew that somehow, someway, she would find the means to do what Jesus wanted her to do.

Chapter Two

The winter had come and gone, and here it was: spring, 1894. New life was beginning to stir on the farms; calves had been born and weaned, the fields had been plowed and seeds planted, and life was pretty much the same it had been for as long as anyone living in Bensenville could remember.

The Harlin's had officially changed the name of their establishment from the 'Harlin Dairy and Farm Supply Emporium' to just 'The Emporium.' After all, this is what nearly everyone was calling the store, so the Harlin's decided to make it official.

On a comfortably warm day early in April, Bill Harlin and his father Isaac were outside The Emporium working on the façade of the store, painting out the old name, and replacing it with the simpler title.

By the way Mr. Ferguson, along with his hired handyman Janos Polchev, were driving the wagon into town, anyone could surmise that there was a problem out on the Ferguson's farm. As the wagon sped by, Harlin shouted out, "Hey Ferguson! You and your boy there need to be a little more respectful to decent folk around here. Some of us are law abiding citizens."

Janos jumped from the wagon even before it came to a stop and headed in as few strides as he could to Dr. Wesson's office. As soon as Jim Ferguson was able, he tethered the horse pulling the wagon to the post between The Emporium and Dr. Wesson's office. Without a moment's hesitation, Ferguson strode menacingly toward Harlin, who was still perched on his ladder.

"Harlin, do you have a problem, or are you just one bona fide idiot?"

Harlin was not one to forego a challenge, so he climbed down the ladder to confront Mr. Ferguson. "We could settle this now, Ferguson! That is, unless you prefer settling it with the rest of the Party."

"I'm not afraid of you or anyone else in your so-called 'Party,' Harlin. What Janos and I are doing here today is not any of your business. But, if you decide to make it your business, we can make it all our business and get it over!"

Isaac Harlin could see that Ferguson was not in the mood to back down. This looked like something that the Party was going to have to deal with, and soon. With nothing else to say, Harlin gave a wave of dismissal and stalked off.

At that moment, Janos and Dr. Wesson hurriedly came out of the doctor's office, the doctor racing towards his buggy, and Jason returning to Mr. Ferguson's rig. Somewhat out of breath, Janos said in a guttural voice, "We must return to farm! Doctor, follow quick!"

And, with that, the two horse-drawn conveyances left the town as quickly as they had entered, the doctor following Mr. Ferguson. All those who watched what had taken place were unaware of why the doctor was needed so urgently. Of course, most who were watching all that had occurred guessed that Mrs. Ferguson was needing the doctor's help, but then why would the hired hand go to fetch Doc Wesson? Wouldn't Ferguson do this himself? It was obvious that the young immigrant was needing the help. Since it was apparent that this was a problem for someone that they all felt was outside their circle of concern, most of the so-called good people of Bensenville thought nothing more of it.

A very worried and fearful Janos paced back and forth in the sitting room of the Ferguson's home. The doctor had been with the young, extremely ill and expectant Soninka for at least twenty minutes now. Janos wanted, with all is will, to go to his wife and make everything better. He was a man of action and will, and to find himself utterly at the mercy of another person, even though that person was a trained physician, seemed to go way beyond his endurance level.

Mr. Ferguson, who was trying his best to calm the young man, said,"Janos, I know this is difficult for you, but you must have faith that God is smack dab in the middle of all this. What, with both Doc Wesson and Nora helping her, Soninka cannot do anything else but make a turn for the better."

"Ano, ...Yes, Mr, Ferguson. My mind say yes, Mr. Ferguson, but heart say, no!"

"Don't doubt God, son. He has brought both you and your wife so far. I cannot believe that you will not see his mighty hand at work."

"I pray you correct, Mr. Ferguson. I pray, so hard."

At that moment, Nora Ferguson came out of the bedroom carrying a pan filled with blood-stained cloths and water. There was a concerned look on her face, but at least the two men did not see any defeat or dejection in her eyes. The doctor followed her out and gently closed the door behind him. Mrs. Ferguson was going to stop and have a few words with her husband and Janos but decided to concede any comments for the doctor to discuss with Polchev. As Nora continued out of the room to take the pan and towels to the kitchen, Doctor Wesson stopped before the men and cleared his throat.

"Gentlemen, I think we had a close call here. Mr. Polchev, your wife was hemorrhaging quite profusely, and quite frankly, she has lost a lot of blood. It is uncertain as to whether or not the baby is still alive, but at least the bleeding has subsided, and your wife is resting."

"My God, Doctor! Is bad, no?"

"It's bad, yes. But there's been worse. Your wife needs to remain quiet for the next week or so. She needs to remain flat on her back, and as inactive as she can possibly be. Unless there is another bout of this type of bleeding, I will be back in about a week to check in on her again."

"Yes, Mr. Doctor. May I see Soninka now?"

"Sure, Mr. Polchev. Please, just let her rest as much as she can. You've got to help your wife as much as you can. Given that, I don't see why you can't have a healthy baby."

Janos shook the doctor's hand, mostly because he did not quite know what else to do. "Doctor, I take good care of Soninka."

And, with that, he quietly slipped into the room where his wife was resting.

Once the young man had left the room, Doctor Wesson confided with Ferguson, "Jim, she just about lost that baby. I'm serious. She needs as much rest over the next few weeks as she can get."

"Got it, Doc. We will make sure that Soninka and her baby are kept safe and sound. You can count on it."

With that, the doctor left, and Ferguson went into the kitchen to help his wife.

Under the cover of darkness, a small group of men gathered at their new meeting place. Harlin knew that it would be safer for what the group were planning if they could meet somewhere away from the normal ebb and flow of traffic in town. His unused and empty outbuilding at his house would perfectly meet their needs. So, as silently as possible, the men who had started referring to themselves as the Home Guard began assembling in the vacant barn-like structure on the Harlin property.

"Okay, Isaac. What brings us out here tonight?"

"Listen gents. Don't you agree that this immigrant problem has gone just about as far as we can allow it to go?"

At this inquiry, several of the men chimed in their agreement.

Harlin continued, "I don't think, deep down, that we can really blame these people like that Polchev couple staying just a small piece from my very home. After all, each and every one of us want something better for our own."

George Lawson quipped, "Okay Isaac, so what in the world are we here for?"

"George, you've got two young'uns, don't you?"

"You know I do, Isaac. What are you getting at?"

"You've told me how much trouble you have keeping them from eating all of the cherry pie that your missus makes."

"I believe my two children could eat a ton of sweets."

"Why don't they, George?"

"My wife and I don't allow that, Isaac."

"Just my point, everyone. Listen, these immigrants are coming here in mass because a lot of otherwise good people are helping them find what they're looking for. I guess some might say that they are enabling them."

All the men heartily agreed.

"So, don't you men agree that people like Jim Ferguson and his wife are enabling these people? If it weren't for the Fergusons and others like them, these foreigners would have gone back where they belong a long time ago."

There was a general consensus among all the men; they agreed that everything Harlin had said was absolutely right. They also wanted to know what he specifically wanted to do.

"Men, we all know that what we have to do is awful desperate. But desperate times require desperate measures, as they say. I think it's time that we send Jim and Nora Ferguson a message that they will never be able to ignore. I believe that the little building of theirs that they are allowing those Russkies to stay in needs a little make-over. Nothing that a couple of well-placed matches wouldn't take care of."

Harry Withers, another one of the disgruntled members of the Home Guard, said, "Isaac, I'm with you one hundred and fifty percent! We gotta' do something, and I think this is a good start!"

The rise of unchecked anger and emotion is mighty contagious, and before long, the men hastily began to formulate a drawn-out plan. A couple of the men brought some hard liquor, and before long, most of the men were imbibing the alcohol to steel their courage. Within forty minutes, talk was turning to action, and the group quickly turned into an angered mob. This, in turn, became a small group of vigilantes with malice in their hearts as they exited the building to converge upon the Ferguson farm.

Jim and Nora Ferguson were enjoying the company of Janos and his wife Soninka. They were like the children that the Ferguson couple never had. After a great dinner that Nora lovingly prepared, all four were seated in the Ferguson's parlor discussing the events of the past few weeks. Of course, the discussion soon focused on the near miscarriage that Soninka experienced.

"Soninka, Mrs. Ferguson and I were so worried for the two of you. We both know how devastating it would be to you if you lost this baby. Please, please, please, know how much we have been praying for you."

"Mr. Ferguson, I know how much you care for Janos and me. You are so kind to us, and you have both sacrificed so much."

"Oh, Soninka, ...Sophie, you don't know how many blessings we have received by helping you two, or should I say, you three."

Nora could see a slight look of disappointment in Soninka's eyes. She asked if maybe there wasn't something that was troubling her.

"Mrs. Ferguson, I have become like sister with Sara Harlin. I am saddened because I have not seen her lately. I think maybe I, how to say, offended her."

"No dear, that's not it. Sara is a good and dutiful daughter. Mr. Harlin has forbidden her from having anything more to do with you. I know she so much wants to come here to be with you, and especially now, with all that you are going through. You just need to know that Soninka."

Janos, who was listening to all that had been said, finally added, "Mr. Ferguson, Mrs. Ferguson, as my Soninka say, you are much like parents to us. You give us so much and we would not last without you both. You are true picture of Christ to me."

"Janos," Mr. Ferguson replied, "We have always done what we know the Lord wants us to do. I know you are still searching for the answer that we have found in Christ. Mrs. Ferguson and I are praying for you to find the peace that Jesus gives."

"Thank you, Mr. Ferguson. I feel I have answers soon, and ..." Before Janos could finish his thought, the flickering of fire began to bleed through the window. And then the sound of celebration emanating from outside began to filter into the parlor of the Ferguson home.

Jim ran quickly to the nearest window, pulled the drapes aside, and gasped, "My Lord! Janos, your home is on fire!"

Soninka was still too weakened by her condition to leave with the rest in order to investigate what was happening outside, but Janos, Jim, and Nora quickly ran out of the house. Polchev was the first to get to what was now Soninka's and his home, but it was quickly enveloping in flames. As Janos tried to battle his way to the building, the flames' intensity was violently increasing. It was impossible to get any closer than thirty feet because of the heat billowing from his home.

Several times he was able to overcome the severe heat from the flames and almost grasp the door handle in order to force his way into his burning cottage. What reason drove Janos to try to broach the flames and enter the house was only known to the young man. Perhaps it was the only positive thing he thought he could do in this situation. At best, he was only capable of taking a few steps past the door before being overcome by the inferno. Time after time, the force of the flames repelled Janos back out of harm's way.

Soon, Mr. Ferguson and his wife caught up with Janos and saw that trying to put out the fire was a lost cause. They pulled him back away from the burning building, and Mr. Ferguson wrestled Janos to the ground, forcefully restraining him from making any further attempt at trying to put out the fire.

All night long, the Fergusons, Janos Polchev, and eventually his wife Soninka sat far enough away from the flames to remain safe. Silently, they watched everything that the Polchevs owned go up in smoke. Jim and Nora were awfully concerned with how this would affect the Polchevs. Soninka fought back the tears, thinking about what would happen to her small family now that they had lost everything. Janos Polchev seemed to be the only one not showing any emotion at all. Staring stoically into the embers of what had once been their lives, he had a grim, set and determined expression on his face. It seemed that some thought or question that continued to plague him had finally been answered.

Mr. Ferguson could see that Janos was more angered than he had ever seen him before. He spoke as calmly as he could, "Son, I know who was behind this. We can let the law handle it. Trust me, Janos, all will be well."

"Trust? Trust who, Mr. Ferguson?"

"Janos, we have laws in this country against this sort of thing. I know that Harlin is behind this, and there are plenty of men who came out with him tonight who will buckle under the pressure that I intend to use against them. They will spill the beans, and Isaac Harlin will be lawfully prosecuted."

"I think not, Mr. Ferguson. I think is all hopeless."

Nora added, "There is nothing hopeless with God, Janos."

"I see here how your God works. This God you worship. I think maybe this God does not like immigrants much. Thank you for all you have done, Mr. Ferguson. Janos must take care of Polchevs!"

At those words of dismissal, Janos stalked off, intent on distancing himself as much as possible from the others. Soninka seemed to be determined to follow after her husband, but in her weakened condition, all she was able to do was summon the strength to reach the gate through which Janos passed into the night. She knew her husband well, and stared silently, with tears streaming down her cheeks, as Janos silently disappeared into the darkness.

Three weeks later, in early May, Ferguson made his way toward the post office in Bensenville, when Isaac Harlin suddenly confronted him on the covered boardwalk. The smirk on Harlin's face was nearly all that Jim Ferguson could take. Once again, Harlin had gotten his own way, and innocent people had to suffer for that. Janos and Soninka had lost all that they own, and now Janos was nowhere to be found. It seemed that Soninka was going to have to raise this expected baby without her husband's help.

Meanwhile, Harlin continued to spew his vitriol, while at the same time sitting among the saints at his church, listening to messages about Christ's love. Harlin needed confronting, but Jim was not sure he was up to confronting the man without feeling anything but hatred towards him.

Harlin stepped up, as if to cut Mr. Ferguson off, and sneered, "So, Ferguson, are we learning anything about what's what?"

"Harlin, you need to just keep away from me!"

"Keep away from you! I've got a right to be wherever I want to be, Ferguson."

"What gives you the right to be anyplace you want to be when you deny other people the same right? Why do you think you are the one who should decide who has the right to be anywhere?"

"I don't suppose I know what you're talking about. As long as you're an American, you've got a right to be anywhere you want to in this country."

"Harlin, you're so full of your own importance that you can't see the difference between what's right and what's wrong."

At that, Ferguson pushed Harlin away and continued his mission to retrieve his mail. Gus Norton, the clerk behind the counter, greeted his friend Jim Ferguson and asked how everything was going since the fire.

"As good as anything can go after a major portion of your property is burned to the ground deliberately, and nothing is done by any law around here to investigate the crime."

"The sheriff isn't doing anything?"

"Only telling me that there's not enough proof. Says he's looking into it, but it just seems like Harlin's got more people working for him than those at the Emporium. Anyway, ...could you check my mail for me Gus?"

"Sure thing, Jim."

Within a few moments, Gus came back from the mail bins with two or three envelops.

"I don't know, Jim, but it looks like you have a letter here from Janos."

Jim took the letters from Gus and walked over to a desk where he could open the letter to see if it was from Janos. After a few moments, he made a beeline from the post office to his wagon, and then back to his home.

"Nora! Nora!" Jim yelled out as he hurriedly entered his home. "Nora, where in the ..."

"I'm right here, Jim. What in the world is wrong?"

"Nora, where is Soninka? I have something for her here."

"I think she's in the back somewhere. She's looking through the remains of their things. I think she still hopes to find some clue about where Janos might have gone."

"Well, go get her, Nora. I think I've got the answers for her right here."

Without hesitation, Mrs. Ferguson quickly ran out towards the back of the house to fetch the young girl. In what was hardly any time at all, Nora returned with Soninka on her heels.

"Now, Jim, what on earth?"

"Nora, you won't believe what came to me in the mail. Really, I should be saying that Soninka will not believe what we have received."

"Mr. Ferguson, what is that you have received?" Soninka asked.

Handing Soninka a letter with handwriting he could not decipher, Jim Ferguson said, "Gus, down at the post office, gave me our mail, and this was in it. I certainly cannot read it Soninka, but I can read that it should be something that you might want to read."

Carefully reading the return address, Soninka exclaimed with an outburst of glee, "Is Janos. Oh, dear God! This letter from my Janos!"

"Well, open it dear!" offered Nora, with nearly as much excitement.

And Soninka did just that. The more that she read, the more the excitement arose within her and on her face. She could not contain the joy that was welling up in her, and finally, she burst out, "Mr. and Mrs. Ferguson! Janos is fine. He is just in Chicago. After he left that morning, he left directly for Chicago. Is working now and wants me to join with him. I must go to husband!"

"Soninka," Nora exclaimed, "Wait! What kind of job does Janos have, and where will you live?"

Rereading the letter for more details, Soninka finally replied, "Yes, here it is. Workers for the Pullman Palace Car Company on strike. Janos say workers needed, and new workers might get jobs. Janos went to work for Pullman Company and has secured housing from his job. He say is good house. Good for new baby to soon come."

"He's working in place of the striking workers?" Mr. Ferguson joined in. "Soninka, he's a strike breaker. He's being used by the railroad company to keep them going during the strike. It's dangerous Sophie. I'm sure that it may be unsafe for the both of you."

"I not sure what you say, Mr. Ferguson. All I know is that Janos wants me to come be with him. I cannot refuse! I go. Tomorrow, I go!"

The next morning, Sara Harlin was busy at The Emporium, stacking small goods for sale in a display outside the front. As she was sorting through the goods, she saw the Ferguson wagon drive past the store. Mr. and Mrs. Ferguson were seated up on the driver's seat, and Soninka was sitting back in the bed of the wagon. Along with Sophie, she also saw two or three suitcases.

The Fergusons pulled the wagon up to the train station that was at the end of Central Street, as Sara saw the three on the wagon disembark and gather the luggage as they were getting ready to go to the ticket office. Sara wanted so badly to run to the depot. She wanted to contact the one who she felt she had betrayed. She knew what her parents, especially her father, would do but it did not matter. Without another moment's hesitation, Sara ran to the train station to see her old friend.

Just ahead of her, Sara saw the Fergusons and Soninka walking up to the passenger platform. Sara bounded the steps and had caught up with the three in no time flat. One look at Soninka, and young Sara Harlin broke into tears of remorse.

"Oh, Sophie, I am so sorry. I have been such a fool."

"Sara. Sara. What, ...where have, ...Sara, I have missed you so much!"

"Soninka, ...Sophie, I have been such a fool. My father threatened to throw me out if I so much as mention your name to him anymore. He forbade me from having anything to do with you. Now, it seems that even my own brother, Bill, has taken up with Pa's sentiments also. Sophie, my whole family is wrong, but I refuse to fall in with them. You are my best friend Soninka, and I love you like a sister."

"We are sisters, Sara. We are sisters in Christ."

They fell into each other's arms as two sisters who had been absent from one another for years. It was then that Sara was cognizant of how Soninka's pregnancy was fully showing by now. "My, Sophie! There's no denying that you are going to be a mother real soon."

"Yes, Sara. Baby comes soon. We have much to talk about but is too bad. I go to be with my Janos now. He is at work now with rail car company in Chicago. I think the name of company is Pullman Palace Car Company."

"Oh Sophie, that is such good news!"

"Yes, is good. I go live with Janos in Chicago. Not far from here. You come soon Sara."

The train sounded its final boarding horn, and Sara said with a teary voice, "Sophie, I will miss you so much. Please write me to let me know where you live so that I can visit soon."

They hugged each other one last time. Mr. Ferguson quickly helped Soninka onto the train and handed her the two suitcases which contained everything in the world that she owned. Soninka and Sara reluctantly waved goodbye to each other as the train slowly but surely pulled away from the station. Tears rolled down Sara's cheeks as she realized that it would be another long while before she saw Soninka again.

Unknown to Sara, her brother Bill had been watching all that had been taking place on the passenger platform. In disgust, he shook his head and a sinister glare began to grow on his face.

Chapter Three

"The Windy City," "City by the Lake," "Second City," and "White City!" These were the common terms of endearment for the city on Lake Michigan, but to everyone else it was best known as Chicago. But the city that everyone in the Midwest looked to for hope and inspiration was developing growing pains of its own.

The closing of the Columbian Exposition the previous year was accompanied by a severe depression that hammered all of the industries in the United States. The hope that the World's Fair inspired was quickly shattered, replaced instead by the reality of hopes lost and lives eroded. Laborers on the railroad and all the companies that depended on the railroad, such as the Pullman Palace Car Company, were adversely affected. Jobs were lost and workers were desperately trying to organize themselves into unions in order to preserve all of the hope they had as they looked forward to a better future.

In the area east of Cottage Grove Avenue, between 103rd and 115th Streets, the community of Pullman, Illinois was annexed into the city of Chicago just six years prior. This was where Janos and Soninka Polchev, along with everyone else who worked for the Pullman Palace Car Company, lived. Each and every one of these company employees were afforded a home to live in, and the

Pullman Company was more than happy to take the rent from these workers, of course as part of their salaries. As the depression continued to take its toll on the nation, Pullman tried to help their bottom line by cutting wages, laying off workers, and maintaining the same rent structure from before the economic downturn. These were the conditions that the Polchevs found themselves in at the beginning of May, in 1894.

The din of the hammers and grinders was deafening, and yet Janos continued the task set before him by his supervisor. Last week it had been much easier for his crew to complete their quota of installing the beds in the luxury cars of the Pullman Sleeping Cars. But last week, his was a crew of eight men, and now they had been reduced to just six. The same amount of work was expected to be finished each day by three-fourths the number of men. Janos and the five remaining laborers were hard at work installing the velvet, plush and ornately cushioned bench seats in the car they were assigned to finish on this day. To break the monotony of the task at hand, Janos and Marek Dušek chatted about what was becoming the most talked about topic.

"So, Janos, you are not having trouble to put food on table at home?"

"Marek, you know that we all are having struggle. Who is not?"

"Who? You know who Janos. Men in office with fancy clothes, Janos, that's who!"

"I am happy to work, Marek."

"This is better job for you than before?"

Janos remembered how much he had grown to love the Fergusons, but he also remembered how much the rest of the town hated him for something that he would never understand. He came to this newly adopted country of his with high hopes. He used all the proper channels and procedures to get into America, and now just because he might not sound the same as everyone else, or because he had a foreign sounding name he was rejected. Was this to be his lot in life? Would he always be outside, trying desperately to get in? He wanted to work; he wanted to contribute; and he wanted to be respected for his attempts at these things. But there always seemed to be others who made it their life's purpose to squelch his efforts to achieve his dreams.

"What do we do, Marek? It seems that even as we work harder and harder, we continue to slip farther and farther back."

"Haven't you heard the men who have been talking about the union, Janos?"

With a sudden expression of fright and looking around to see if anyone had heard his friend, Janos extended his hands out to try to silence Marek's interjection. "Marek be quiet. Such things are bad to talk about here!"

"What Janos? We cannot talk? Soon we will not be able to breathe, my friend."

"Marek, we must be careful when we talk. That is all I am saying."

"That is all anyone says," Dešek stated in exasperation. "I am thinking, Janos, that we are quieting ourselves into death. We need to stand strong together, Janos. If some will not stand with us, it might be too bad for them!"

"What do you mean, Marek?"

"I mean that more trouble may come for workers than from bosses!"

"You are trying to frighten me into what I may not want, Marek. This talk may not be good at all. Not good at all, Marek!"

At that, Janos left the interior of the car the two had been working on and took a turn at a task in which he could work alone.

The apartment on 105th Street was a far-cry different than the little home that Janos and Soninka had made for themselves on the Ferguson farm. It was by no means built for coziness or comfort. Strictly speaking, it was more for profit than for quaint epitaphs of "Home Sweet Home."

Still, Soninka had spent the past couple of months after arriving in Chicago to be with her husband, making their little squalor into something that might bring joy to her tired and weary Janos. He spent long hard days at the Pullman Factory, building luxurious coaches that wealthy travelers would be able to rest comfortably in as they traveled.

She felt so bad for her poor Janos who worked so very hard for he and his wife, and now his soon to be born child. Every week after toiling for sixty or more hours, he would be so happy when he laid down the nine dollars he received in earnings. She often wondered how long it would take him to purchase a ticket to ride in the very same train cars that he was paid so cheaply to build. After all, some of these wealthy patrons of the railroads thought nothing of paying upwards of sixty-five dollars or more to make the short trip from Buffalo to Chicago. Poor Janos would have to work seven weeks just to afford the ticket for that ride. That would be a long, hard seven weeks unless he wanted to pay for things like food and a place to rest his weary body each night. Then, it would take even longer for Janos to be able to ride the very cars he was building.

But still, he was a proud man, and so happy that he could bring enough money home to afford this meager dwelling and put some substantial food on the table. She worked as hard as she could in order to make his life bearable after a long shift at the factory. The one thing that she was determined to do was at least provide him with a clean home, good home-cooked meals, and some semblance of dignity.

Now, as Soninka was busy putting the final touches to that night's meal, she could hear the bright whistling of Janos as he was passing down the hallway towards their apartment door. The metal-on-metal sound resonated throughout the room as she heard him opening the locked door. There was never a time since arriving in Chicago that Soninka was not reminded of the risks everyone face living in a crowded, and sometimes crime-ridden section of the city. Door locks were a necessary fact of life for everyone.

She smiled though, knowing that her young, strong husband was now home after spending twelve hours at his work. As the door opened, she quickly went to greet him with a kiss that welcomed him into his home. This she could give her husband. This she knew no one could destroy or take away from them. They may be struggling to create a life that was more than mere existence, but she knew that her strength was found in both her faith in God, and in her love for her Janos.

"Good day this day, husband?" she asked as she helped Janos remove his work boots.

"Ano, ...yes, my dear wife. This be a very good day. Yes, very good!"

"Janos, you sound excited. What is it that makes you this happy?"

"It is about work Soninka. It is about being able to make better life for my wife and my child soon to be," he said as he set his boot over to the side and out of the way.

"I do not understand, Janos. What is making it better?"

"I did not want you to be, how do you say, ...oh, yes, to worry. Last month there are some men who joins the union of workers. I talk with Marek this day about what is happening. He tell me that workers try to form what he called, uh ... union."

"Yes, Janos, I have heard of this thing. How does this mean for you?"

"For me, my dear, this is good news. Company say, need for men to work in place of those who decide they not work! They do what is called, 'strike'!"

"Janos, you still have job even with this, this strike?"

"Better than that, Soni. I have raise!"

"Raise! More money?"

"Yes, my dear. Not just raise. I get better job, too!"

"What better job, Janos?"

"The trains still need handlers and porters. This means more money. More than three dollars each hour higher than what Janos earn now. Soni, life is better now for you, and for baby. I am so happy now, my dear."

Soninka wanted to be happy. She wanted more than anything else to make Janos feel like she was happier than she had been in a very long time. But something deep down in the back of her mind was troubling her. Maybe it was just the fact that she wasn't too keen about sudden changes. Their little life together was going as smoothly as it had since coming to America. This news from Janos seemed to portend all sorts of anxiety within her.

Her mood quietly lifted when Janos held out a letter that he had picked up at the mailbox when he came up to their apartment. She could see from the return address that this letter was like some sort of unexpected gift. It was a letter from her dear friend in Bensenville, Sara Harlin.

Quickly, she grabbed the unexpected letter away from Janos and retreated into the bedroom to read it. She read what her friend had to say:

"My dearest friend Sophie,

"I am so sorry that it has taken me these two long months to write to you, but I had to be sure that prying eyes would not see to whom I am writing.

As you probably guessed, both mother and father are still quite against me having anything to do with you. I pray for them every day, but it seems that my prayers go unanswered. At any rate, I am so happy to get these few lines off to you.

"Mr. and Mrs. Ferguson are both doing as well as any can expect. They both miss you and Janos terribly.

"I have made friends with a missionary couple who are working at our church. Their names are Steven and Joan Merra. They both work so hard, trying to serve our little community, but it still seems like many of those who call themselves believers are hesitant to show Christian love to others.

Here is the news I've been wanting to tell you so much. The Merras are wanting to go to Chicago to do some summer missionary work, and they have asked me to assist them.

"Sophie, I now know that God truly works in mysterious ways. When I brought the subject up with my mother and father, they both have agreed that I can do this missionary work with the Merras. I don't know. Maybe they both feel guilty about not keeping their promise to bring me to the Exposition last year.

At any rate, I am going to be able to see you very shortly as we will be coming to Chicago in the middle of May. One of the things that Steve and Joan want is to work with the poor laborers in the city. "Sophie, please write to Mrs. Ferguson to let her know where you live so that I can visit you soon. I plan to spend a lot of time catching up on everything. And, I really hope that I am there when your baby is born.

"I give you all of this in love and encouragement, "Your very dear friend, Sara"

Tears of joy flowed down Soninka's face as she read and reread this letter to herself. She was so happy that she would soon be seeing her dearest friend in the world.

After seeing to it that Janos had his dinner, she sat down quietly in her room, took out a sheet of paper and a pen, and began writing, "Dear Mr. and Mrs. Ferguson," ...

Janos stood, looking at the others that had been called to the foreman's office. Each of these men shared one thing in common, a great desire to work hard in order to provide for their own family.

There was very little else that any of these forty-four men gathered outside Joe Regalt's office shared with each other. They spoke their own native tongues, ate their own perspective types of food, and very few of these men shared a common culture. A couple were Irish, three or four were Italian, and a handful were American citizens because of an amendment put into force only twenty-four years ago. But a vast majority of these workers had immigrated from the villages and towns of Eastern Europe. They were from places such as Servia, Montenegro, Romania, and Eastern Rumelia.

Two other very important things these fellow Pullman laborers held in common were a desire to work hard to improve their lives, and a fear of association with some type of labor organization. This sort of thing never worked out so well for them in their native lands. Nearly all only understood one thing – honest work. At best, they felt that joining together with others to force the owners to give into their demands seemed to be dishonest.

Joe Regalt, the short and burly foreman of Janos's work group came out of his office carrying a clipboard and a no-nonsense attitude. Joe had earned the respect of these men gathered there due to his hard, but straight-up nature. When Joe said a thing, that thing was law. He was tough but fair, which was something these hard-working laborers respected. Joe was strict and demanding, but he also demanded the same from himself as he did from those who he led. This was something these men could understand and respect.

"Listen men," Joe began, as he firmly addressed these workers. "I know that some of you are a little bit concerned about what's going to be happening to your jobs around here in the next few days."

A general murmuring rose among the men as it seemed that Joe had struck a chord among them all.

"I want to assure each of you that the Pullman Palace Car Company is very appreciative of your loyalty to the company. Each of you can be certain that you will not be losing your jobs."

"Whut about the threat we're a hearin' frume those over in the ARU, sare," came an inquiry from McGyuire, a ten-year veteran of the Pullman company.

This interjection for the Angus McGyuire caused the small crowd of laborers to break into a small din of questions and accusations.

"Yeah, will listen to me all of you!" Regalt asserted. "Those men are scum, and they are cowards! They're no better than a pack of jackals. That Railway bunch – you know who I'm talking about – the American Railway Union, they are nothin' but bullies, and you all know the only way to match a bully is by banding together and outsmarting them."

The murmurings subsided somewhat, but still the more forceful of those in the group wanted to know how their families were going to be protected if they decided to stand up to the union members and keep working through the strike.

"Okay, okay! Let me tell you all something." Joe shouted out over the growing surge of questions. "Listen men, I am not going to stand here and tell you that this will be an easy thing for you to do. You are going to have to decide for yourselves. Do you want a job with Pullman or not? We are going to stand firm against the threats of this ARU, or whatever other organization tries to bully its way into our business."

"So, vhat ve do, Boss Man?" asked one of the men standing next to Janos.

"Okay. Here it is." came the answer from Regalt. "From what I understand, on May 11th there is a call for the railroad workers, and anyone else who supports them, to go out on strike. That is this Friday, men. If you are here and ready to work, then you have your job. If you don't show up, then, well, don't ever show up again. Is that understood?"

Again, there was a small murmuring of dissent and questioning among the men. Some were still concerned for the wellbeing of their families because of veiled threats by the union members. Others were voicing a fear for their own safety.

Joe could sense that some of the men's fears were beginning to escalate. "Guys, listen. I'm not going to tell you that this will be easy. I'm not even going to say that you will not have to face retribution from others in the community that don't even work for the railroads. I know as well as you that at least half this city is on the side of the union's demands. But, let me give you a little bit of information that may help. We all know how dependent this country is on the flow of goods across this country. If somethings going to be sold in San Francisco, then it has to be shipped by train. President Cleveland is well aware of the need for the flow of product throughout this nation. In the end, Pullman Company and the railroads are going to be protected by the federal government. That's a mighty powerful force on our side gentlemen. So, do not let these socialists gain a foothold in our country because of fear."

Some in the crowd of workers quieted down. Others still asked questions to each other about their concerns and doubts.

"I hope to see each of you here on Friday," Joe finished his little address to the men and walked back into his office, closing the door behind him.

Janos looked around at those who were still gathered there. Some, he knew still had unabated doubts and fears. Many were determined and settled about what they would do. Quietly, two or three at a time, the men began to filter out of the factory. Janos knew that he was going to be here on Friday. He was not about to let others scare him into compliance with their own agendas. His wife Soninka and their soon-to-be newborn child needed him to remain brave in the face of any danger. He would work!

Chapter Four

The three passengers aboard the eastbound train from Bensenville were excited as their train began slow down while it neared the depot in Chicago. Both Steven and Joan Merra were thrilled that they were about debark from this train and begin a work they had been talking about and planning for more than five years. They were both certain, after much prayer and discussion that this is exactly where God wanted them to be.

They had been making the circuit throughout the villages and cities in Illinois and as far as into most of the states that bordered. They had made the circuit into the churches and Christian fellowships in all of the places they traveled to, appealing for funds to help them establish missionary work among the poor immigrants in Chicago. Granted, not many people in the churches they visited were as enthused about this mission as they were. Some claimed the calamitous times and the depression the nation was going through was enough reason for them to withhold any support for the Merras' work there in Chicago. It is very easy, even when Jesus addressed this very thing about money worries and cares of the world in his Sermon on the Mount, to let these cares overwhelm you. Steven and Joan knew that. It was forgivable, because they knew that even they had wrestled with allowing the cares of the world overwhelm themselves.

But what filled the couple with sorrow was those who were considered to be highly respected and also well-blessed by God who were never hesitant to interject their own brand of what the Bible said or did not say. They were never shy about stirring up uncalled for fear and even hatred among many of the parishioners of the churches they approached for aid during the past five years. The young missionaries could not understand how it was perfectly fine for some people, whose grandparents or even parents had made their way to this country from their homes in Ireland, Scotland, or Germany, and to settle in and make this nation their own home. But for some reason, these people could not afford the very same privileges as those who sought the same means for liberty. It was bad enough that these people took upon themselves to interject their own interpretation of the Word of God, but they compounded their folly by making themselves self-appointed gatekeepers of what God did or did not say.

Nevertheless, the young missionary couple had the support from true believers that they needed to minister to those in need, albeit later than they had expected, and with far greater opposition that should ever have taken place. The next step on this benevolent mission was to get things organized in the little abandoned storefront building they were renting from the Illinois Central Railroad.

Rumors were abundant about the stirrings going on within the rank and file of the workers. There were many honest but poor people who, although they were being used as pawns by both the railroads and the unions, wanted nothing more than to take care of and feed their children. These men and women who just wanted to work and provide a place of freedom and opportunity for themselves were being pulled in two directions. The railroads were threatening them with the loss of their jobs if they fell in with the union, and the union was issuing veiled threats of violence towards anyone who dared to cross the picket lines, should a strike occur. That innocent people would have to be forced to make a no-win decision such as this was unacceptable in the minds of these two young missionaries.

Sara, on the other hand, was filled with completely different feelings as the train was making its slowing course into the Grand Central Station on the shore of Lake Michigan. As was customary, the train was ending its deceleration with bells sounding out warnings of coming to a stop at the platform, and the billowing steam from the boiler of the engine car issued out around the first three cars of the local that ran from Chicago outward to the outlying towns and villages of eastern Illinois. Although the actual trip from Bensenville to Chicago was only about an hour, for a young girl of seventeen, with the added excitement of finally getting to see the sites that she had been longing to see for more than two years, an hour felt like an eternity. Sara wondered what she would do when she got to the city. Was she obliged to stay with the Merras for who knows how long? Was she going to be allowed to have some time for herself before too long? And there, at the back of her mind, nudging her emotions, was the desire to make contact with her dear friend whom she had been missing now for more than two months. When and how would she be able to find Sophie Polchev?

"Anxious to see your friend?" the familiar voice of Steven Merra queried from behand Sara.

"Yes, Steven. I miss Sophie so badly. There is so much I want to know. Is everything okay with her and Janos? How are they gettin' along here in this big city? Well, I 'specially want to know 'bout the baby, and how that's goin' for them."

"Well, Joan and I reckoned that it might be best for you to make contact real soon with your friends. We think that once we get everything to the place we've gotten for the mission, well then, you ought to try finding your friends."

"That is so gracious and kind of both you. Are you sure that you won't mind?"

"Nonsense, Sara," Joan interjected as she joined in the conversation between Sara and Steven. "You are going to be reaching out to the very people we came to serve, Sara."

Having disembarked from the train and retrieving everything that they brought along on this mission, the three found themselves surrounded by a sea of fellow journeymen. There were more bodies in the terminal depot than Sara had ever seen assembled together in Bensenville at any one time. It would be no hard task for the three to become lost forever from each other. But with careful coaxing and instruction, Steven, Joan, and Sara soon found themselves and all their possessions quickly portaged from the station to the abandoned storefront that would serve as both their home and their mission of mercy.

Sara was as excited as she had ever been in her life as she jumped from the supply wagon Steven was able to employ back at the station.

"Hang on there, Sara!" Steven said, as he was still helping Joan down. "You're gonna' break something if you don't watch it, and I don't mean something on the wagon. You're gonna' hurt yourself!"

"Sorry, Steven. I'm just so filled with excitement 'bout bein' here."

"I know, I know. But let's get you settled into your room here first. You won't be any earthly good to friends if you end breakin' a leg or somethin' even before we get into the house."

With that, and a deep breath to slow her excitement, Sara and the other two quickly had all their cases and boxes off the wagon and into the building before too long. As Sara and Joan started sorting these things out inside, Steven drove the wagon back to the station in order to return it. By that first evening of June 5th, everything at the mission was miraculously in some fashion of order.

Soninka could hardly hear the knocking at the door. The open windows to help relieve the sweltering heat on this unseasonably hot June morning and the sounds of the busy street outside were drowning out any knocking at the door.

But either the noise from outside quieted down, or the knocking became a little more persistent. At any rate, Soninka, well into the final weeks of her pregnancy, responded to the summons at the door.

What, or who could it be? she thought with some trepidation. The inuendoes and outright threats from the railroad workers towards the men who chose to stay and work rather than go out on strike were now becoming more and more intense. At first, the targets of these so-called 'persuasive' devices had been the workers themselves. Now, the families and homes of the men were under attack. Just about one week ago, Soninka's neighbor down the hall had a package of a dead rat sitting outside their door. This was a less than subtle reminder to the Falccino family of what happens to those they consider to be rats.

At first, the strike was well-supported by nearly all of Chicago, and it seemed that the railroad companies were about to make some big concessions. But things escalated very quickly. The American Railway Union tried to launch a national boycott of the railroad, and very soon, what seemed to be conciliation by the railroad turned into hardening hearts and a change of position. There were many issues literally riding on the trains, as they not only were used to move cargo, but also the mail, which is where it all went badly for the union. The president of the United States, Grover Cleveland, rightly surmised that the movement of mail in the country was essential. So, in response to the strike, federal troops were put on notice that they would likely be used to restore order.

There was no telling what Soninka was going to find when she opened the door. She knew, by the persistence of the knocking, that whoever it was would not go away. So, like one rips a bandage off quickly to get it over with, Soninka opened the door as fast as she could. And there, with an astounded expression on her face stood Sara, fisted hand up, ready to knock again on the door with even more force.

The two young women could only stand there with mouths wide open, as if time had come to a standstill.

"Well, do I have to keep pounding on this door until my hand falls off?" Sara asked, breaking the stunned silence between the two.

"Sara, Sara, ... oh, Sara! I am so sorry," exclaimed Soninka.

Quickly, as the two girls collected their thoughts and came to their senses, they embraced each other as two long-separated best friends should.

Sitting at the small kitchen table, hands clasped together, and glasses partially filled with lemonade, the two young women shared the events of the past three months. "Catching up," as they say, is so very hard to do when there are so many questions that need to be answered. But surely and slowly, Sara and Soninka were able to fill in the missing pieces of their lives that had been so abruptly separated by the heinous vigilante acts of the so-called upstanding community of Bensenville.

"No, Sara, do not continue with bad feeling about sad people in your town. God has answer for our prayer here in Pullman. Janos work good job."

"But Sophie, aren't you scared 'bout all this union commotion? Sounds to me like most o' these want you all dead!"

"Is talk. Is only talk. My Janos say things look good here."

Soninka seemed somewhat unsure as she offered this last comment to her dear friend, and Sara could sense that. It was not too hard to tell that there was a deep-seated fear lying within the heart of her friend.

The two talked about nearly everything that they could think of talking about. Soon, Soninka glanced at the clock in the small living room, and gasped, "My! Oh, my, we have been talking so long! Soon Janos come home. I must have his meal ready."

Sara agreed, "Yes Sophie, I know. But we still have so much to talk on. You know that since I am now working here with the Merras, it will 'ford me more time to visit. I want to be here for your birthin' too."

The two embraced one last time as Sara left, determined to come back and somehow convince her friend to at least come and see what was going on at the mission. After all, that is what it was there for – to serve people just like Sophie and Janos.

Later that evening, Soninka began to worry about Janos. It was later than he normally took to return home, and he had not mentioned having to work later. Her imagination began to create many scenarios about why he could be so late in returning from work. Part of her knew that he could take care of himself if any one person decided to take up matters hard-handed against him. But deep down inside, she knew that those who posed any threat were too cowardly to do so without plenty of help. This was not the first time that the scenes of her worst imagination played out in her mind. What would she do if anything untoward happened to her husband? What about the baby? What could she do? She knew that some of the other young married women whose husbands were either killed or mysteriously missing were unable to stay in the homes they all had to rent from the Pullman Company.

And still, she could hear the ticking of the clock, each tick portending some measure of doom. Her husband was dead; no, her husband had to work overtime. But this hour was way beyond what overtime would be needed. Back and forth she went, and as the minutes turned into four hours, she was beginning to feel a discomfort in her abdomen that was bordering on shooting pains. Now, she knew that something was not right. It was not right with Janos or their unborn child.

Finding some relieve for the surging spasms in her belly by lying still in bed, Soninka did the best she could to also quiet the rising hysteria of her mind. And when she had reached the point in which she felt she would surrender herself to full-blown panic, she heard the front door quietly open.

"Who is there?" she asked, hoping that it was who she expected.

"Who are you thinking is here, my dear Soni? And where is you?"

Trying to rise from the bed to greet her husband, Soninka felt a sharp sensation as if a knife was ripping its way through her lower belly. She gave out a sharp gasp and scream, causing Janos to burst through the bedroom door to find out what was wrong. It was then that Soninka saw his bloodied face and torn clothing. With another gasp, she passed out, nearly falling out of the bed, causing Janos to run to her in confusion, not knowing what was wrong with her.

"She's going to need to be kept quiet," the summoned midwife told Janos. "The stress of what she was going through today, not knowing whether you were alive or dead, has devasted her. She did nearly lose the baby, but if she stays lying down and if you ken keep her comfortable, well, it's a good chance that things will work out right."

Janos's face showed a dark expression as he looked at his wife.

"But listen, Mr. Polchev, you probably need to be seein' a doctor yourself. You look like you been tended to with a hammer and saw. Looks near like you need some stiches and some bandagin' for those wounds. What in world happened to you?"

Janos did not want to discuss his afternoon with anybody, let alone this woman who was an expert at delivering babies, but probably not a labor relations expert. It seemed that as soon as his shift at the Pullman Company ended, he was confronted by four men who he knew were on strike. Before too long, words became action, and he found himself in a dire situation of having to fight all four of these men. He could certainly have handled them one at a time, but that was not how they settled things. By the time they were finished pummeling him with clubs, he could hardly see through his swollen eyes. The loss of blood also caused him to pass out as he tried to cover the distance from the railyard to his apartment.

"I'm thinkin' that maybe you need t' call in the law. This might be a matter for the police, if ya ask me."

"I think maybe you do not know much of this. I think law is no answer here. Law help striker much but workers fend for self."

"But Mr. Polchev, right is right, and no one has the right to do what they did to you no how."

"I thank you Miss Barkley. You good midwife. I take care of Soni, and she stay abed. Police no help Janos. Police side with union. You go now. I call again when time for baby be born."

At that, the midwife dismissed herself and left. As his wife tried to rest and find some sleep, Janos sat by her bed with his mind buried deeply in his own thoughts. Somehow. he must be able to live and to work and to survive for these two people he cared for more than anything else. He must be there for her, to provide for her and to keep her safe. Somehow, he must be vigilant and never be caught unaware again. He must be vigilant.

Sara's days were filled with many things to do, and time, which passed ever so slowly as she was waiting to come to Chicago, was now speeding by like an express train from New York City.

It was now the first day of July and it seemed that the entire city was preparing for Independence Day celebrations. Banners were hung on the street posts and building facades. Occasionally, at night, the sound of pistols would resonate through the neighborhoods. The police had warned people not to fire guns within the city limits, but how in the world were they ever going to stop it? With all the worries about the trains and the loss of wages since the beginning of the strike, people were searching for ways to blow off a little steam. It had been almost two months since the strike began, and both patience and pocketbooks were wearing thin.

Fortunately for Steven and Joan Merra and the mission they had started, the newly formed Central Relief Association was more than willing to sanction their work. Week by week, more people came to The Harbor of Light, as they called their work in Chicago. Through donations that were coming in at a quick rate, and through the strong support of the CRA, Sara soon found her days filled to capacity with helping those affected most severely by the strike and boycott that was beginning to gain steam.

There was always something to do at The Harbor, and Sara found it more and more difficult to get away to check in on the Polchevs. Her days were filled with the tasks of sorting donated clothing items, helping Joan and the new kitchen staff volunteers prepare the evening meals that would be served to hungry families, and to help sort out and distribute the many household items that were desperately needed in Pullman City.

Sara, however, was feeling an incessant urge to get away from this much-needed work and find her way to Sophie's apartment to help her dear friend in any way that she could. She was more than worried about her friend, who had grown to be more like a sister than anything else. During the past two months, it was not uncommon for Sara to be seen at the Polchev's, bringing them the things that were being distributed there at The Harbor. What with the extended hours that Janos was being asked to work, and the fact that Sophie was bed-ridden, Sara was able to convince her mentors, Steven and Joan, to let her take these items to the Polchevs.

Sara grew more and more concerned about her friend, Sophie. Day by day she could see her becoming more and more frail as the worries about the safety of her Janos and the quickly approaching birth of their child began to take its toll on the young immigrant woman. Sara tried to ease Sophie's concerns about her husband because she just knew that this was the chief reason for her waning health that only served to threaten the unborn child. Whenever Sara could find the time to visit with Sophie, she could see the increasingly worried look on her friend's face each time footsteps were heard in the hallway outside their apartment. She knew that her friend was afraid that the next passerby was a harbinger of news that would bring her world to an end.

Today, Sara would try to calm Sophie by sharing a letter she received from the Ferguson's back home. In her heart, she knew that Sophie was needing a touch from others that she had grown to love and trust. Maybe this letter would bring her some peace of mind.

As had become an accepted custom between her and Sophie, Sara rapped on the door of the apartment with her customary three knocks, a pause, and then another three knocks. She opened the door, which was kept unlocked in case someone needed to get to Sophie in an emergency, and called out to her, "Sophie?"

The silence from within the apartment filled Sara with some trepidation and anxiety as she opened the door wider. Usually, Sophie was quick to answer when Sara called out upon entry, but today, the response was silence, and that worried her.

Again, she called out, "Sophie!"

A muffled whimpering was all that Sara could hear, and it sent terror and an electric rush through her heart. Something was wrong! Quickly, she headed straight to Sophie's bedroom, and found her lying on the floor next to the bed. Sophie was struggling to get up but was failing at every attempt.

"Sophie! What? ...Wait, don't keep trying to get up. Let me help you!"

Rushing over to her friend, Sara found a hidden source of strength and was able to lift her friend from the floor and ease her back onto the bed. Making sure that Sophie was secure from spilling out onto the floor once more, Sara made her way to the kitchen and returned to her friend's bedside with a glass of water.

"Sophie," she said after giving her a few sips of the water. "Sophie, are you okay? What were you trying to do? Why were you on the floor?"

"Můj manžel, myslel jsem, že má potíže,"

"No, Sophie, Sophie, in English Sophie."

"My husband, ...Sara, oh Sara, I'm so afraid for Janos. Sara! Is not good. Janos in danger. Many threats. He is not know how much. Sara, Sara ..."

Sara saw that Sophie had drifted off to sleep. She was more than concerned for her friend. She was also terrified for their unborn child. This fear that Sophie was going through could not be good for either her or the baby. She also took a closer look at the face of her now-sleeping friend. It dawned on Sara that she had not really examined her friend's condition with anything other than cursory looks. Now she saw that Sophie was not doing very well at all. The face she looked was drawn, and pale. Her friend, who was so strong just months ago, seemed to be fading. She looked so frail as she fitfully slept, probably dreaming about what might be happening to her husband.

As she looked upon the face of Sophie, tears began to seep from Sara's eye. What could she do to help her? Could she go to the police to make a complaint for the couple? She could already answer that question. It would be a waste of time and effort. There was only one thing she knew that she could possibly do. Holding Sophie's hand, Sara closed her eyes, and began silently praying to God to bless her dear friend and to protect the yet, unborn child.

The celebration of the Fourth of July had come and gone, and now the city was returning to the grim fact that, although the nation had just commemorated the 118th anniversary of the nation's birth, trouble was still at hand. Quarrels and debates concerning the strike were still at the center of everyone's thoughts. Violence seemed to be breaking out all over the city about this issue.

To take her mind off her fears and anxieties, and maybe to help Soninka endure until the expected day the baby would be born, Janos was planning a great surprise for his sickly young wife. This had been an extremely difficult time for her, and the young father-to-be, wanted to ease her worries over all the threats over his decision to forego the strike and to keep working. It was Friday night, he had just gotten paid, and so Janos decided that he would bring home something special for Soninka's dinner this warm July 6th evening. He thought that he might try to find a way to get to "The Pump," as everyone called this eatery, but it was more than eleven miles from Pullman City, and there was no way that the food would be worthy of his precious wife's consumption. Besides that, the fifty cents he would need to pay for their two dinners, and the fifteen cents that it would take to buy the dozen or so pieces of "Reed's Butterscotch Drops" that Soninka seemed to crave would deplete his weekly wages too much. All it would do is probably give his wife another burden to worry about. But thank God for the saloon down the street from the factory. Five cents for the cost of a beer, and the bar would throw in a free lunch that could serve as a dinner. Janos reasoned that a couple of different visits to two of the laborers' favorite saloons might procure for Soninka and himself a much-needed respite from their steady fare of sauerkraut on bread they had been having for the past couple of weeks. He would then be able to stop on his way home at the little candy store and pay for the dozen or so candies. A wonderful surprise for his wife at a cost of a mere quarter!

The whistle sounded through the factory, signaling another end to the workday. With a smile on his face as he contemplated the joy he and Soninka would have that night because of the little surprise he had in mind. Janos bounded out the doors of the factory, heading towards the tavern two blocks away. His thoughts were on how happy his dear Soni would be when he came home with his dinner surprise and the sweets. He was so happy about his plans that he did not even notice the shadowy characters following him with clubs and knives. Even though the bosses and the companies hired "industrial police" to help break the strikes, these thugs who conspired with the unions were no better. They were not beyond using any, and all means of intimidation to coerce the "scabs," as they called the ones who had decided to cross the picket lines, into submission. That is just what this small band of hired bullies were about to do. They would make certain that another one of the many foreign scabs would be certain not to be able to work again, whatever it took. If they were a little more exuberant with their methods, well, that was just the price that had to be paid for taking away the jobs that belonged to good, upstanding union members.

Without a worry in his mind at all, Janos slipped into the saloon to at least pay the nickel needed to grab the greasy fish and oily fried potatoes at the end of the bar. Wrapping it all up in a piece of wax paper, and neatly placing the half-warmed bundle of food in his lunch bucket, Janos headed out the door, seeking another establishment where he could find nearly the same fare. He knew that Jerome's Saloon, next to an alleyway on Stephenson Avenue between 107th and 108th Street, would probably be the best place to find what he was looking for. And besides that, there was the little confectioner's cart on the corner of Stephenson and 108th that usually sold the type of butterscotch candies Soni was always craving.

Janos was so distracted by thinking about his surprise for Soninka that, as he turned into the alleyway in order to enter Jerome's Saloon where immigrants were required to enter, that he did not hear the band of men fall upon him. Had he been aware of them, he might have had a better chance.

It was getting late; more than two hours later than Janos usually returned home. Sara, who had come to visit again with Soninka on that hot Friday afternoon sensed the worry in her friend's face. She knew that she should leave, but she also knew that abandoning her friend now might be far worse than over-staying her welcome. Besides that, she could see the turmoil within her friend's countenance beginning to rise to the surface. Soninka was racked with constant fear for her husband, and it was taking its toll on her health, and probably the health of her unborn baby.

"Oh, Sophie, please calm yourself," Sara tried to comfort the fretful Soninka.

"Is not right, Sara. Is late! Much too late! My dear Janos is too late!"

"You don't know, Sophie. He might have been asked to work a couple of hours longer today. Maybe there is a big new order for product he has to get ready. Who knows, Sophie."

"Sara, I feel something wrong. Deep in my heart, Sara."

"Please don't fret, Sophie. It can't be good for your baby."

"And what is to happen to my baby, Sara? What I do if Janos hurt, or, or, ... oh, Sara, I cannot say what I fear most times now!"

Before Sara could respond in any way, there was a sturdy knocking at the door. Sara was startled somewhat by the interrupting rapping on the door, but she was startled even more after opening the door and seeing the tall, Chicago police officer standing there.

"Sorry to bother you, mam, uh, ... Mrs. Pol,..., uh, Pol-chev?" he stated in a questioning manner, not really knowing if the lady standing there could speak English.

Sara could only stare at the officer, wondering why he was there, but knowing deep inside the probable reason for his visit. Something was wrong and she was afraid. She was afraid not just for Janos and not just for Sophie. No, she was filled with dread for what might happen if, or probably when, the officers delivered terrible news to her friend. Ultimately, she was terrified for the baby.

Coming out of her reverie, Sara responded, "I'm sorry, no. I am not Mrs. Polchev. Sophie, uh ... Soninka Polchev is restricted to bedrest for the sake of her unborn child. Is there a problem, officer?"

"And who are you, mam?"

"Oh, yes, well, I'm Sara Harlin. Sophie and I are very dear friends. Why, we are probably closer than sisters, if you really wanted to know."

"Well, Miss Harlin, what I have to say is for Mrs. Polchev's ears, and I need to ..."

At that moment, Soninka was standing on wobbly legs at the doorway to the bedroom. Holding onto the doorsill, she weakly asked, "Sara, what is police want? Is it my Janos?"

Seeing the young woman standing there, the officer blurted out, "Mam, uh, Mrs. Polchev. I am Officer Reedley, and I am sorry to have to tell you that we found your husband dead, …"

He got no further in his explanation to Soninka. The sound of her falling in a faint to the ground was all that Sara heard as she quickly ran in response and to aid her friend.

As soon as she reached Soninka, she called out to the officer, "Please, please I will take care of her. Just find my friends, the Merras. They run The Harbor down by the depot. You know, the mission there. Please, find them and let them know that I need their help with Sophie. They will know what I mean."

Officer Reedley was a little hesitant to leave, but he could see that the young woman was tending to her friend, and he would just be getting in the way. He saw that the best thing he could do for Mrs. Polchev was to find the missionaries that Miss Harlin requested him to find.

Chapter Five

The small group gathered in the pasture-like setting of Dunning, a small town located about eleven miles northwest of Chicago. The nearby insane asylum loomed in the background, giving an eerie feeling to those who were standing near the two newly dug gravesites. Standing there, all donned in the traditional black of mourning, were Steven and Joan Merra, along with Sara Harlin, who was holding a small bundle in her arms. Thankfully, the week-old baby she held was peacefully sleeping, allowing the other few attendees to hear the words of those who were paying their last respects to Janos and Soninka Polchev. The few there included some of the residents in the small apartment in which the couple had lived, and two or three men who worked with Janos in the Pullman Rail Coach Factory.

Who knew if there might have been a few more to come out to this service to honor the couple if they had been buried in one of the cemeteries much closer to Chicago? But that would have cost much more than the pittance that the couple had been able to save and store away in the coffee tin in the kitchen cupboard. There certainly was not some type of savings or endowment set aside for either one and no wealthy family members had stepped up to defray the cost of a grave closer to where they had been living for the past few months. The best that could be found was this cemetery in

Dunning, which was set aside for those considered to be indigent. Of course, this meant that just a few of the couple's closer friends and acquaintances would spend half the day going to the small, but meaningful service that would mark their short lives.

Silently and tearfully, Sara looked around at the setting in which she would leave her dear friends. It was not what one would ever label as a picturesque setting. But it was quiet, and at least it did afford Sophie, as she called her friend Soninka, and Janos a rest from the worries of this life.

Steven and Joan Merra looked over at Sara, who was holding the newborn child of the Polchev's with tears streaming down her cheeks. Joan remembered the scene in the small apartment the immigrants rented from the Pullman Company. They remembered how Sara was fitfully helping her friend who had gone into labor from the shock of the news that the young police officer had delivered. A couple of days after losing her best friend who was the closest thing to a sister that Sara ever knew, she had found the wherewithal to talk about what had happened after the police officer had left to find her and Steven.

The shock of the news had caused Soninka to go into labor. Sara did not want the baby to be born there on the floor of the apartment, so somehow, she found enough strength to get her friend back into bed and was tending to her as the baby was emerging into life. She could see that Sara was doing all that she could to keep Soninka alive long enough to complete the delivery of a little baby boy. As Joan and Steven Merra finally entered the apartment, they found Sara, in a dazed state of shock, holding the newly born, but surprisingly healthy boy. Lying on the bed next to where Sara and the baby were sitting was the dead body of Soninka. This final assault on the young immigrant woman was more than she could take, and death won out.

These thoughts and remembrances quickly subsided from Joan as the here and now returned to her mind. Silently, she began to consider what was to happen to the child. Certainly, the county of Cook may have had jurisdiction in the matter of orphaned and unnamed babies, but would it really be the best solution to just hand the baby over to an uncaring and overworked bureaucracy? Would that really be a viable solution for what to do with the child? It might make things easy for everyone involved, but would it be the best for everyone, especially the baby?

The missionary couple had spent the last two nights discussing the resolution of this problem. They wrestled with expedience versus the will of God. Yes, it would be quick and relatively easy to just turn the baby over to the sheriff. The child would then be placed in a county-run orphanage, and probably spend the next sixteen to eighteen years as a ward of Cook County. Simple solutions, though, are not always the best. Occam's Razor was sometimes just not the most sensible, especially when it came to matters of the heart. Didn't the Church have a valid claim in cases such as this? And wasn't The Harbor Mission, in a real sense, a church?

As all the mourners at the funeral service wended their way back out of the cemetery, Steven leaned over to Joan and whispered, "You know, we have a really sensitive problem here."

"I know, Steven," she replied, looking at Sara who was carrying the baby just forty feet in front of them.

"What do we do, Joan?"

"Steven, it's all I have been praying about for the past two or three days. I know what would be easy, but I don't think easy is always right. Sometimes easy solutions are not God's solutions."

"I'm thinking the same, Joan."

"Listen dear," she lowered her voice even more. "Doesn't it behoove us, as in fact, leaders of a faith community, to seek do our best to keep this child under God's care and not another case file of the government?"

"I'm certainly glad to hear you talk that way, Joan. Surely there has to be someone in our little community here that can have enough love in their hearts to take in this little child."

"Yes, Steven. At least, as a Christian fellowship, we can act like the church is supposed act and try to make a home for the child."

"Good! Let's talk about this more, and especially with Sara, when we get back to The Harbor."

"So, you're sayin' that we're gonna' try to find somewhere for little Jesse to live for a home?" Sara asked, after laying the sleeping baby in its crib in a small room at The Harbor.

"Have you already given the child a name?" Joan asked.

"I saw no reason he should go nameless."

Steven responded to this, "but Sara, what if his new parents want to call him something else. Aren't you taking that option away from them?"

"The truth is, I can't just go on say hey Baby, or something like Sophie's Baby. That just don't seem right, 'specially when I'm wantin' to talk d'rectly to him."

"Well, it probably don't matter much if we do call him by a name. But Steven and I were both wondering how long you can stay here to see to it that Jesse has a home? This might take longer than you'll be here, Sara."

"The real truth is Joan, ...Steve, I think there be no one ready to take him on. The folks we have been working with in the mission are much worse than can take on a new responsibility of a child."

"You might be right," answered Steven. "So, what then?"

"I'm glad you've broached that subject, Steven. I'm glad it's out there now so we can be preparing ourselves for it."

"Well, what are you thinking, Sara?"

Sara sat down, and began to speak with conviction to the couple, "Truthfully, Steven, I love that child, ...I love Jesse as if he were mine. I was closer to his mother than anyone else, and I feel that I can do the best for him. I think I can lead him into becomin' the young man his mother wanted him to be. I talked so long with Sophie and no one in this country knows more about him than I do."

"But Sara," Joan spoke up, "what about your mother and your father? Are they really going to allow you to bring this child home?"

"I can't rightly say for sure what my ma and pa will do. I know they love me, and I am more than sure they would support me with this."

"Even your father, Sara?" Joan asked.

"My pa? I know he was against Soninka and Janos. I know he felt that they shouldn't be here in this country because they were from somewhere else. But I don't think he can say the same for Jesse."

Sara looked over into the room where the baby was soundly sleeping in his crib. She seemed to be gathering her thoughts. Finally, she spoke again, "My grandpa and grandma were both from Scotland. They came to this country as young struggling farmers and settled in Virginia before the War between the North and South. It was there that Pa was born, a full-fledged, natural-born

American. So, you see, Pa and Jesse have much in common. I think he'll see Jesse as bein' just like him."

Steven thought for a moment before responding, "I believe we should do this, Sara. Why don't we make an attempt to find a home for the child? Why don't we honestly try to see if any of the married couples we are working with would like to be blessed with this baby? Why don't we all take a trip to the county orphanage and take a look at things for ourselves? Maybe we are premature in judging what things are like. Why don't we all do that before we make any snap decisions? Sound right, Sara?"

"Well, I'm gonna' say that it's a pretty sure bet that things is as bad as I think they are. But I don't suppose I have a problem with makin' sure about everything."

Silence could be extremely loud. It seemed that the folks who regularly attended the services at The Harbor had spoken their piece without having to say a word. Oh, there were the usual statements of, "that's so sad," and "I will surely be praying about that," when the subject of taking on and adopting a new baby boy was presented to a few of the families. Some folks were very honest about the hardship that another mouth to feed would present; and it was true for many of the families. Every single person had to work just to survive. There was no time to be spent on caring for an extra 'burden,' so they would say.

For the most part, after being presented with the prospect of taking on this extra responsibility, a few of the members of the church just seemed to drop off the face of the earth. They just quit coming to services. Sometimes avoidance is easier than doing what your heart tells you is the right thing to do.

So, the only other option that seemed proper, at least to Steven and Joan, was to examine the orphanage in Cook County to see if this was a viable solution to the situation. They soon discovered it was much more like an almshouse than an orphanage. They very quickly witnessed that about sixty children lived in what could only be described as more of an institution than a home. Most of these children were attended to by their unwed mothers and therefore were not up for adoption. The hopes for these children were that their mothers would soon be able to take on the responsibilities of caring for their children on their own.

The other children – the ones that were mostly like the young baby Jesse – were the ones that no one would care to adopt. They would be the ones who were so scarred and sickly that no one would even think of bringing into their homes. They would have to learn on their own how to fend for themselves and survive in an ever-growing world of rejection.

Later that same night, as the missionary couple were getting ready for bed, they began voicing what they had been thinking all day.

"You know dear, it all comes down to two things," Steven broached to unspoken.

"What are you thinking Steven?"

"Well, what I'm thinking is the obvious. There are only two options we can take with this child that Sara has taken to call Jesse."

"So, again, what are you thinking?"

"Listen to all I'm saying, Joan, before answering. You know that what most folk would say is the obvious answer is for us to take on the responsibility. You and me, Joan. We're relatively young, we have no children of our own, and we have a stable living situation here, more or less."

"Go on."

"Okay, that's one side. But the other is that young woman on the other side of this house, sleeping with, and caring for that little baby right now. She loves that child as if it were her own. She would give her life for Jesse. Sara would see herself as the mother of the baby, but we would be looking at the child as an obligation. Sara sees the baby as a life that needs nurturing, and we look at it as a responsibility or a burden to carry. Don't you see what I'm talking about Joan?"

"Yes Steven, I do. What the right thing to do does not always depend on how much money you have. Money is not always the best security for a young child. Sometimes the best kind of security is that which comes directly from the heart."

"I think the answer has already been provided by the good Lord, Joan."

"I think you're right Steven, but what about her mother and father, and all of the folks back in Bensenville? How are they going to take to this child in their midst?"

"I believe that Jesse has the best chance to survive there than in the streets of Chicago, Joan. Sara will make sure of that!"

"You know what, Steven? I think we should go tell her. We should go tell her our thoughts right now. And after that, we should, all three, ...no, all four of us – Jesse's part of this – should sit right down and pray for God's will to be done."

Sara sat in the coach car of the train, holding the small baby close to her heart, turning her attention to the couple standing on the platform, waving to the train. Though she knew that they would not be able to see her as the steam billowed out from the engine, obscuring everything, Sara waved back. The train slowly pulled ahead, beginning its journey back to her small village and to points beyond.

Lovingly, she looked down on her little baby. She knew that she probably should have wired or written home about Jesse. She knew that her pa had nothing but hatred for Soninka and Janos, but how could he hate the small little one-month old baby that she was holding in her arms? How could anyone hold so much hatred that they would want to see harm come to anything so defenseless and so precious?

As the train accelerated ahead, gaining speed and heading for her little town, Sara looked again at the now-sleeping child, and she observed the passing landscape, thinking once more about the life ahead. Through her doubts and trepidations, she kept telling herself that everything would be all right.

Chapter Six

Mr. Isaac Harlin was indeed a very complicated man. He claimed to believe the teachings of the Bible and the words of the apostles and was always one of the loudest voices extolling the virtues of love and brotherhood. But, as they say, what you see is not always what you get. It's awfully easy to espouse brotherly love and the virtues of "giving water to the thirsty," when it isn't directed towards oneself. It's easy to be a whole-hearted, "dyed-in-the-wool," Bible-thumping agent of God when you didn't have to show your true hand. Nearly everyone knows that when a person plays poker, they can always bluff if they are only holding a pair of twos. But walking-the-walk, in faith, was a far sight different that playing a hand of cards, where you must play the hand you are dealt. In matters of real faith, all believers are holding aces galore, and they are all called upon, from time to time, to show their hand.

Mr. Harlin showed his hand, and what he was holding was hate. He not only hated others, but he made hate an artform. To all he dealt with, in his daily business life, in his civic duties in the town of Bensenville, and even in his position as deacon of the First Community Church, he was the picture of saintly devotion. But it was all a mask, or better yet a contagion. He affected many of those around him. For reasons unknown, Isaac Harlin was a man of which many people did not want to be on the wrong side. Having the only farm supply store in a farming region meant that Harlin could substantially harm your livelihood, should he choose to do so if you disagreed with him on anything. Being one of the more successful businessmen in the town allowed him to be able to give a vastly greater sum of money to the First Community Church, affording him whatever power he wanted to wield in that body. His money also bought him plenty of clout with the local law enforcement and political agents in the county. Isaac Harlin was indeed a powerful man, and he used his power to get whatever he wanted for himself, or whatever he decided that any other person would need.

One might expect that Mrs. Harlin would be a kinder, more reasonable, and a more accepting person. One might expect that, but one could be very wrong in thinking she would be any different than her husband. Both of Sara's parents had developed a hardened heart when it came to those they felt were not "one of them." It could be said that Anne Harlin did wish that her daughter would come to her senses, and she knew that if Sara did begin to see things their way, then things would be just fine. It saddened her heart that Sara was so rebellious towards her and Isaac, but at least their son Bill was much more in line with their way of thinking. And this gave her solace during those times when she thought about the strained relationship between Sara and her. Besides, Sara was young and naïve, but she would see the light; Anne was sure of that.

Sara would soon find out how hateful and powerful her father truly was. Her return to Bensenville at the end of the summer in 1894 was not exactly what she anticipated it would be. Really, she did not know what to expect from either her father or mother, but she did not expect what she received.

As she disembarked from the train at her arrival back in Bensenville, she could she the icy expression on her father's face, as he waited in the carriage that would convey her and the baby she held in her arms. She did not know what to expect, but she certainly did not prepare for the stone-cold silence that she received from her father. No hug from him, no offer to retrieve her luggage, only a hard and rage-filled stare was etched on the man's face. Silently, Mr. Harlin stepped down from the carriage and moved to the baggage claims dock to retrieve his daughter's luggage and trunk.

Wheeling the load on a small hand truck, Isaac Harlin silently loaded the items onto the small area behind the carriage seat. Climbing back up into the driver's seat of the rig, Harlin said, as he stared straight ahead, "not a word, young lady. I don't want to hear one word from you about why you brought that foreign child back here. We will talk about this back home."

The silence of her father was loud indeed, but the icy cold reception she received from her mother and the equally silent rebuke from her older brother spoke volumes. The ultimatum from her parents was simple and forthcoming; Sara was welcome to remain in her parents' home, but never would they allow Jesse to remain there.

Her father's lectures left no doubt as to what was expected from her. They would purchase a ticket on the next train back to Chicago. She was to take the child with, and deposit it at the county orphanage, as she should have done when it was born. There would be no argument from her. These were the rules that were laid out for her, and if she had any intention of returning to the Harlin home, then she would fully comply – end of argument!

This is what found the young, now-homeless Sara, making her way with silent tears streaming down her face and carrying both her two-month-old infant and a makeshift rucksack down the dusty path away from the Harlin house. Jesse was her child now and not the ward of the state; there was no way she was going to turn her baby over to a cold, heartless institution where he would grow up with zero nurturing and guidance. When she was given the ultimatum from her father and mother, she knew that any amount of pleading would fall on deaf ears. She had to get out of that house and leave everything her parents could claim behind. She gathered the few garments that she obtained from working with the Merras in Chicago, wrapped them up in a discarded tablecloth her mother was throwing away, picked up Jesse, and walked out of the house of Isaac and Anne Harlin, never to return again.

Sara desperately tried to think of where she might go. She had to at least find a place of refuge until she could sort things out. For no reason at all, she thought of the Fergusons. She had never really known Mr. and Mrs. Ferguson at all, except only as customers at the Emporium, but she did recall that they were the ones who took in Sophie and Janos back before they went to Chicago. She could not rightly remember why the young immigrant couple had left Bensenville, but she had heard, during the early Spring, about a fire at the Ferguson farm.

Sara knew that Mrs. Ferguson seemed to act towards Sophie more like a mother than a landlady. It might be, Sara reasoned, that the Fergusons were kind of like surrogate parents to the Polchevs and would be awfully excited to take in their young child and herself. It would never hurt to try to find out.

And that is how Sara and Jesse became residents at the Ferguson farm. There was no hesitation on the part of Nora and Jim Ferguson to offer a home for the two of them. It would have been nice if the burned-out building was available, but it was still in disrepair. Nora Ferguson told Sara that they had a spare bedroom in the house that she could set up as her own, and if and when Jim got Soninka's and Janos's old burned-out building fixed up, then Sara and Jesse could move in there. Now that he had a reason to begin fixing up the damaged that had been done to the building, Jim reassured Sara that it would take no time for her and little Jesse to get settled in.

Sara could not believe that people who were nearly strangers to her would show such openness and love to her and Jesse. But as she spotted the opened Bible at the table where Nora Ferguson usually had her cup of coffee, she had some inkling of understanding. She had never experienced this level of love and acceptance from her own father and mother, but in some way, she knew that this is what true Christian love is all about.

The days, weeks and eventually months passed as Sara and Jesse settled into their new life in Bensenville. Getting into the routine of living this new life on the farm with her close friends Jim and Nora Ferguson became such a joy to the young woman. Sara treasured the relationship she was building with her new friends. They really felt more like parents than friends, and Sara was enjoying the time that she had with them, learning more and more about how to live a true Christian life. To spend the evenings just visiting with Nora and Jim, and learning their insights on life, was something that Sara treasured deep in her heart.

Sundays were very special days at the Ferguson farm. Going to church every Sunday morning was a foregone conclusion in her new life with Jim and Nora. It was true that her parents were regular attendees at the Mt. Zion Community Church, but for Isaac Harlin, church attendance was, at best, nothing more than what was expected of him. This was the church that all the most prosperous business owners in town attended. At church these business associates of Harlin's could make the proper connections that would guarantee the success of their little empires. For Isaac, it was his best way to maintain control over what other leading citizens of Bensenville thought and did. But in doing this, he was not much different than any other up-and-coming prosperous entrepreneur could do in order to hold as much sway over their fellow citizens as they could. For these men church was more about networking than about ministry.

The believers who met at the Third Avenue Christian Fellowship were cut from a completely different fabric. There was not any pride or arrogance wafting through the congregation on a Sunday morning service. As the mostly itinerate laborers gathered together, they would lift up their voices in praise to God singing the older hymns, such as O God and Father, Thee We Bless and Let All Together Praise Our God. But they could also be heard in chorus as they sang newer music; the likes of which were forbidden in the statelier churches in town. These recently composed songs were considered heresy by many of the other fellowships. They would never have songs such as Abide with Me ('tis Eventide) or Wake the Song of Jubilee. Even an anthem such as the new America, the Beautiful was never to be heard in those more ancient houses of prayer. There were members of Mt. Zion who felt it was their job to stand guard over what music could or could not bellow out of the organ pipes. Just as Mr. and Mrs. Harlin watched over who could or could not enter their divine sanctuary, these keepers of the hymn books stood vigilant watch over all things musical in their church.

At the Third Avenue Fellowship the attitude was all about living what you sang about. So, if they sang "Come, you nations, join and sing, to the throne your praises bring; let it sound from shore to shore: 'Jesus reigns forevermore'" in Wake the Song of Jubilee, they really meant it with complete sincerity. The song was not just words to fill an empty space, but they were declarative statements of faith and resound.

To the extent that the hearts of these people at Third Avenue Fellowship were full of love and mercy towards one another, their pockets and account ledgers were void. They were mostly the side of society that the people over at Mt. Zion would turn a blind eye to and accuse of having brought on their own misery. They needed the poverty of those outcasts of society to feed their own pride. They could point accusing fingers and complain about 'those kind of people' at Third Avenue Fellowship, but deep down inside, they knew their own societal position was built on the backs of 'those kinds of people.' In short, any kind of help, as far as being able to find viable and suitable employment, was not going to be found among her fellow members at Third Avenue Fellowship. In order to find work that would support Jesse and herself, Sara would have to find it from people who considered her and the baby not worthy of being helped. It was not so much that they thought of Sara in that way, after all, she was the daughter of a prominent businessman in town—even though she and her parents were estranged. The real problem, as they all saw it, was that child of the foreign couple. To most of the crust of society in Bensenville, the baby should be a ward of the state, and nothing more.

The Fergusons were beginning to feel the weight of Isaac and Anne Harlin's wrath. The Emporium supplied all the needs of every farm and ranch in the region. It was no secret to anyone in

Bensenville, especially to Isaac Harlin, that Sara was now living with the Fergusons in the little shanty that he had tried to burn down just a year earlier. Regretfully, with the help of some of those people over at the Third Avenue Fellowship, Sara and her young ward had a nice, safe, and warm place to survive the winter and early spring of 1895. But now, it was time for the farmers in the area to do their planting. Harlin was determined that Jim Ferguson had seen his last days as a successful farmer in Bensenville. Not one thing would be available for him to purchase; not a seed, not a tool, not even a spool of thread for Nora Ferguson to do any sewing. Anything that Jim and Nora needed now would have to be purchased from Chicago and that would require traveling the twenty-five miles necessary to obtain those staples. Jim's health was steadily declining since the fire incident the year prior and the distance to the city would take nearly a full day, considering the fact that he had just two reliable draft horses he could depend upon. Jim Ferguson would pay dearly for interfering in Isaac Harlin's family matters.

Sara saw clearly what her father was up to, and it filled her with both disgust and remorse. The only one placing a wedge between her and her parents' relationship was her father. He was the one who stubbornly refused to have anything happen other than in his own way. As long as Jesse was still around, her father would continue to make innocent, loving people suffer. This both angered and saddened Sara. Jesse was her child now, and nothing would make her turn him over to government authorities. But she could never abide with having the Fergusons suffer needlessly through her father's wrath. For her, the answer was simple; she had to leave Bensenville.

But where could a young, soon-to-be 18-year-old woman with a nearly one-year-old baby go? Going back to Chicago was one option, but to Sara, this was not nearly far enough away from the tentacles of her father. She could not think of any advantage for her if she headed east. There would probably be even greater opposition and prejudice for her and Jesse in all points east or south. She remembered hearing several people talking about a mine out west in the state of Nevada. People were all a-buzz about this place they referred to as Comstock and Virginia City.

The Fergusons felt somewhat dubious about a young woman and baby being able to find safety and security in such a wild, and often-times violent part of the country.

"But Sara, why are you thinking about taking little baby Jesse to such a risky place and Nevada?" asked Nora, as they were discussing what Sara could do to help.

"Nora, I don't think our stayin' here is good for you or Jim. With how my pa's treatin' you two, and now how he's treatin' the rest o' the folk at Third Avenue Fellowship, I suspect it can't do much but get worst."

"Oh, darlin', we've been through hard times in the past."

"But Nora, the hardships that everyone in the Fellowship is suffering, the ones that you and Jim are goin' through, they're directly attached to me. If it weren't for me none of you would be goin' through what you are."

"What do have in mind to do, Sara?"

"Been thinkin' long and hard 'bout that, Nora. Lookin' over all my prospects, it seems the best thing to do is head west. I'd already heard 'bout a place out 'n Nevada. It's a place that's been up and runnin' since the War 'tween the States. Customers who came into the store talk somewhat 'bout it. I believe I recollect them callin' it Virginia City."

"I've heard tell about that place, Sara. It sounds a might bit wild for my taste. Are you sure you want to take Jesse into that?"

"Long as my pa don't know nothin''bout where I am, well, I just think that it might indeed be the best for both of us."

"What are you thinking you might do when you get there, Sara?"

"I'm not certain just yet. There has to be something better than takin' up space and makin' it hard for those I love. Anything has got to be better than watching my pa ruin the lives of those I love!"

"I suppose you're right about that, dear. I just don't want to see you take the path of most young and pretty girls do when they are unaccompanied out in the west. Sara, you don't know what temptations lie out there for you, especially since the two of you would be alone. I fear that out of desperation, you might have nowhere to turn to find work except in either the saloons or the brothels."

"Mrs. Ferguson, ...Nora, I 'spect the most I learned 'bout livin' a Christian life has come from you. You and Mr. Ferguson, ...you both done taught me to depend on the Lord. I know that Jesus will meet all my needs, Nora. I will not be alone, you know that."

"Yes dear, and I also know that you are a strong and faithful young lady. I know you have done nothing that would make me suspect anything other than that. If that is where you feel the Lord is taking you and Jesse, you can know for certain that our thoughts and our prayers are completely with you."

"I really do feel that it would be best for both Jesse and myself, and especially the kind members of our church," Sara responded to the Fergusons.

"Well, dear, it isn't a whole lot, but all of the fellowship took up a love offering for you and Jesse. We want to see that you are able to get started out in Nevada. All toll, it comes to around $250."

Seeing that Sara was going to turn down the money, Mrs. Ferguson continued, "Dear, you need to accept this in the name of the Lord, you understand? It's our way of helping you and the baby. Don't deprive us of this blessing Sara."

With tears beginning to flow down her cheeks, Sara gratefully accepted the envelope Nora was holding out to her.

Sara and her small unofficially adopted son Jesse sat smiling and waving out the window of the Union Pacific coach passenger train. There, on the depot platform, stood Jim and Nora Ferguson, also waving back in bittersweet response. The older couple certainly did not want to see the two leave, but they also knew that there was really no alternative. Hate is mighty strong weapon, and unfortunately, Isaac and Anne Harlin, Sara's birth parents, had hated the small baby she embraced so much that she had no alternative other than to abandoning everything behind to make a safe home out in the unknown. As they stood there, both regretting what was and what could have been, silent tears flowed down the cheeks of both Jim and Nora Ferguson. In the year that had just passed, Sara had become a child to them they were never able to have themselves. And Jesse, for all intents and purposes, was truly their grandson. This would be the last time they would see the two in this life, and the parting was a pain that would require them to forgive the only one responsible – Isaac Harlin. God would need to give them the grace to be able to offer that forgiveness to such a vile and hateful man.

Some of these very same thoughts were on the mind of Sara, as the train began its journey out of Chicago to points west and eventually to Omaha, Nebraska. Her itinerary was simple enough: she would travel out of Chicago, westbound on the Pacific Limited, No. 21 at 10:00 in the morning and arrive in Reno, Nevada at 7:45

two mornings later. In Reno, Sara would need to find an affordable room to stay for the night. Then she would need to catch the Virginia & Truckee, or as it was commonly called, the V & T Railroad passenger train for the last fifty miles of her Virginia City destination. Overall, this would be an arduous three-day journey, especially considering the fact that she was traveling with a one-and-a-half-year-old baby. Everything she owned was jammed into a second-hand steamer trunk that the members of the Third Avenue Fellowship were able to give her, and this trunk would eventually reach Virginia City with or without her. Despite the circumstances, she was fairly confident she would reach her destination without too many difficulties.

The miles of track passed beneath her and the train, and all seemed to go as smoothly as it could. Sara and Jesse made the right connections and finally, as advertised in the timetables, arrived in Reno two days after the 'new phase of her life,' as she called it began. Just one leg remained in her journey to her new, sight-unseen destination. She was to traverse the remaining twenty-six miles, meaning she had about a day or so left.

Sara's biggest concern was locating suitable lodging for the night. She would need to find an inexpensive place that was not too far from the depot. She had to make sure that she would be able to make the final connection on the V & T Railroad at 7:55 the next morning. It was now about breakfast time, and she really needed to get some decent food into her stomach. After several inquiries, she found that one of the best places she might try was the Riverside Hotel. She would only need to walk a block or so along the street the depot until she reached North Virginia Street. After that, she would head south for three or four blocks on Virginia Street, cross the Truckee River using the Virginia Street Bridge, and she would happen upon the Riverside Hotel. She was assured that she could find a good place to eat and a room that she and Jesse could stay in that would not cost a tremendous amount.

Sara followed the directions she was given and by 10:30 that morning she found herself facing the Riverside Hotel. It stood there before her as an eight-story, imposing structure, daring her to seek shelter from what she assumed would be an inferno of rising heat of the mid-summer day. Of course, it was nowhere near as tall as the buildings she had seen in Chicago, including the Delaware, the Home Insurance, and the Rookery Buildings, but there was just something about the setting that made this hotel seem colossal. In Chicago, Sara was quite used to seeing a tall skyline, but here in the middle of mining territory a building this tall was something she was not expecting.

She was very doubtful, after looking at what appeared to be a luxurious hotel, that she would even be able to afford a dinner there, let alone a place to find rest and a good night's sleep. Surprisingly, the prices were less than what the hotels in Chicago charged. For less than two dollars she was able to rent a reasonably comfortable room for the night.

It did not take her long to find rest from the long and weary journey she had just experienced during the past forty-eight hours. A small breakfast, and a good wash of her face and hands did wonders for her weary heart. She was a bit worried that once she lay her head down upon the soft, billowy pillows on her bed that she would drift off to sleep leaving Jesse unattended. But she really had nothing to be concerned about because the boy had also needed a nice bed to find his own rest also. Both Sara and Jesse were almost instantly transported to their world of dreams and much-needed rejuvenation.

By 2:00 o'clock, Sara rose from her morning nap, woke the young child sleeping beside her, and began getting ready to do a little bit of sight-seeing around Reno. This was not her final point of destination, but she wanted to become a little better acquainted with her new surroundings, as it were.

Making sure that she had her room key in her possession, she and Jesse left their room and made their way down to the lobby floor. After everything that people back east told her, she was expecting to be baked to a crisp by the mid-afternoon summer sun. Instead, she was quite pleased to find that, according to the temperature gauge behind the check-in desk of the hotel, it was only about 90 degrees, and it was close to 3:00 o' clock in the afternoon.

The clerk at the desk noticed her looking at the thermometer and asked, "Warm enough for you miss?"

"Really, I was 'xpectin' somethin' quite a bit warmer than this."

"From back east, Ma'am?"

"Yes, Chicago area."

"I think, ma'am, that you are going to find things out here a whole lot different that folks tend to tell. I don't know why, but people always exaggerate how hot it really gets out here. When I came out here from New York back in '73, I remember people back there telling me that the whole place is nothing but some God-forsaken desert."

"I heard lots o' that from people back in Bensenville, ...oh, that's the small town way outside o' Chicago. They seemed like they's tryin' to save me from a fate worse than death. Tryin' to make me feel like I might be burnin' up out here."

"Well, let me reassure you. The temperature you're feeling now is about as hot as it's going to get. And I can also assure you that we do have our fair share of snow here in this area during the winter.

Once you get used to the weather out here, well, I don't think there's anywhere else in the world any better than here in Nevada, ma'am."

"Well, you might just be right. At least I'm hopin' you are," Sara replied as she awkwardly adjusted the one-year-old Jesse in her arms and headed towards the door.

"Excuse me ma'am, are you going anywhere in particular?" asked the clerk.

"Just goin' back over the river to see what there is to see."

Seeing how burdened she was with the baby, the clerk responded, "If you would, ma'am, I might be able to help you with tiny little load you're carrying."

Stepping back into the room off the side and behind the counter, the clerk emerged a few seconds later pulling a utility wagon. Much like a miniature Mormon Cart, Sara saw the advantages of being able to use this cart to carry Jesse while she did a little sight-seeing. The cart was somewhat taller and more durable than a child's wagon, but it wasn't so massively large that it would be a hinderance in her journey about town.

"We use these carts for our room maids to carry fresh linen about from room to room," the clerk said. "It saves a considerable amount of time and trouble for the room servants in accomplishing their daily clean-up."

Sara saw a pile of towels and some sheets that she could use to prop up little Jesse. This would also give him a chance to see some things around the town, and to get a bit of fresh air. She thanked the clerk, from whom she learned was Sam Colden, and placed Jesse in the cart with plenty of support from falling out as she traversed the brick-paved roads of downtown Reno.

Sara and Jesse made their way out of the hotel to see some of the city. She pulled the small utility cart with her baby son aboard, out of the hotel lobby and headed north towards the Virginia Street Bridge and back into the area of town near the train depot. Slowly and surely, Sara was taking in all that she saw. Clearly, this was not what she had been used to seeing back east in Chicago. Out in the distance she glimpsed at the mountains rising above the surrounding flat desert-like scrub. Where she was used to seeing the various greens and yellows of the crop-yields, she was now witnessing many different earth tones of browns, ochres, and reds. Just about the only place she could see any naturally growing vegetation was along the river that wended its way through the city of Reno and continued out into the desert landscape. She realized that where farmers back in Illinois and Iowa made their living from the top of the soil, the miners out here in this part of the country harvested the wealth that would be found beneath the ground.

Looking around for the first time since having a decent amount of rest, Sara could see that what she thought Reno would look like and what it really looked like were worlds apart. Many of the buildings housing the businesses of Reno were of brick rather than the wood that she had seen in the illustrations and images of the postcards and textbook drawings from her days in school. The streets of Reno were also paved with brick, but not to the extent that they had been in Chicago. Of course, Reno could not boast of the abundance of street traffic that Chicago could, but things were well on their way towards every form of public comforts that she could find back east.

As she walked along, keeping a watchful eye on both where she was going and any references to the Riverside Hotel. She certainly did not want to get lost on her very first night in Reno. One thing that was quite noticeable to Sara was the abundance of brick. It was used not only in the street paving, but it was also quite commonplace in the buildings she passed on her way into the business region of the city. She had no idea that because of two disastrous fires just twenty years or so ago, the city made it mandatory for all new buildings to be constructed from brick. Now the brick made in Reno had become quite an institution.

Walking down the raised sidewalks of the thoroughfares, Sara stared in awe as she passed many of the establishments. She carefully read the names on the building; establishments such as the Reno Mercantile, which stood stately across the street from the train depot from which she had arrived. Other sites she saw included the Santa Fe Hotel, a huge home on Court Street. It was not just a home, but a mansion. The corners of First and Center Streets stood the Majestic Theater and the Reno City Hall.

As Sara and Jesse made their way quietly and carefully through the region of the depot, a sudden commotion came along East Commercial Row. Seemingly out of place, and a throw-back to thirty years prior, Sara could see a broken-down wagon pulled by two equally broken-down horses making its way to the Southern Pacific Railroad depot. Seated on the driver's bench, Sara spotted two rough-looking men, both hunched in their seat. The team driver was intent on pushing the draft horses on toward their destination at the depot. The other man was busy reaching back towards the cargo being hauled on the wagon. He seemed to be pulling a rope taut on their cargo which appeared to be furs of some kind. Sara could only imagine the animal these furs once adorned. Yelping and barking out as it followed directly behind the wagon was a brown, black, and white spotted mixed-breed dog. To the young woman this was truly a composition of contractions. Here, in this city verging on the advent of the twentieth century with the modern conveyances of occasional trolley cars and the gas streetlamps, it was quite a shock to see this throw-back to the distant past.

As the afternoon continued to journey through the town, Sara and the now wide-awake Jesse trudged down West Street and happened upon another edifice which declared that even though a rare occurrence such as the skinner's wagon appeared, Reno was on the cutting edge of progress. There on the corner of two well-traveled roads stood a building which she could clearly see was a school. Sure enough, the sign above the front door of the building announced that his was Central School.

It was nearly 6:00 o'clock in the evening, and the pangs of hunger began to gnaw at her stomach. Even though it was nearing nightfall, there was still an abundance of daylight left, as it had barely been a month or so since the first day of summer. The tantalizing aromas of the restaurants and saloons were emanating around and in front of her, pulling her toward Fulton Alley. Turning down this thoroughfare of small dwellings, sheds, and wood piles, there were also businesses such as the Pacific Brewery and Soda Works. The most enticing smells came from a sausage factory called National Market. This was clearly a place that tired railroad workers and others found respite from a hard day's labor. Still, it was important for Sara to keep her mind on her surroundings. Lively music could be heard as it rolled out of the windows and doorways of the saloons and the less-than-respectable establishments. It would not be hard to become a victim or a target of someone's inebriated condition.

She was so deeply concentrating on what lay ahead for her that she did not hear the commotion coming her way. A young, apparently well-to-do, and obviously drunk man stumbled out of one of the more darkly lit bars. One might say that he stumbled out from the saloon, but, in reality, he was in the middle of a sustained fall.

Sara's quick reactions and her steady hand on the cart in which Jesse was reclining, was all that kept him from becoming seriously hurt. She pulled the cart back deftly and turned it just in time for the drunken young man to barely miss it and hit his head soundly on its wheel carriage. The commotion caused by this young man's staggering and subsequent fall could not help but refocus Sara's attention on the moment at hand. There, lying at her feet and now bloodied by the collision with the baby's cart, the drunken twenty-something-year-old young man was trying to pull himself up off the ground, to no avail.

Finally, managing to pull himself up off the ground, and precariously keeping himself balance, the young man slurred out, "I beg y'pardon mam. 'Scews me fo nearly doing you in there. The name's Sanders – Phil Sanders. If I have 'njured you at all, pleez, contac m'father in Virginia City,"

At that he stumbled off again, with blood flowing down the side of his face, and headed towards the Santa Fe Hotel. Sara wondered if she should catch up with the young man to make sure that he was not seriously hurt but stopped when she saw him duck into another saloon halfway down the alley. He would surely be feeling the wound tomorrow morning, she thought as she turned back to one of the nearest cafes for dinner.

Chapter Seven

Sara sat looking out the window of her V & T Railroad passenger car as it headed out of the Reno depot. She was deep in thought about the young man who nearly bowled her over in the alley. She remembered that he had called himself Phil Sanders, but really, all she could remember about him was how obviously drunk he was at only 6:00 o'clock in the evening. She was always intrigued by the stories of others, especially if they seemed out of the ordinary, and she was somehow drawn to this young man she briefly encountered the night before. She wondered what his story could be.

One by one, the train passed through what were called towns but were little more than a few buildings, all seemingly centered around another "Dead Eye" or "Big Strike" Saloon, or some other mine-related nomenclature. Slowly but surely, the pathway that the tracks followed from Reno to Virginia City resembled a "fish-hook" that began in a southerly direction, the slowly curving eastward and eventually northward. By train, they would cover nearly fifty miles, but the distance from Reno to Virginia City was just shy of twenty-four miles as the proverbial crow flies. But this was a train, and it was necessary to follow the tracks that had been laid out for it. The little outposts of Andersons, Browns, Washoe, and Franktown came and went before the train diverted toward the east at Carson City, the Nevada state capital. It did not take long for the view from the train began to change from low-lying desert scrub and white dusty flat land to a much more hill-laden region. The valley gave way to the foothills of the Virginia Mountain Range of western Nevada. The train passed through other little towns that serviced the miners working in the higher elevations including Brunswick and Merrimac. Finally, making a sharp turn back northward, they passed through Eureka, Hayward, Belcher, and at last reaching Virginia City.

Virginia City itself was witness to the mass amounts of wealth that were pulled out of the ground in the form of both gold and silver. Sara did not know too much about the city she was on her way to, but she had heard that the wealth from the silver and, of a little less importance, gold had nearly helped to finance the government during the four years of the Civil War. Millions upon millions of dollars had been pulled out of the mines here in western Nevada, and those still prospecting were hoping against all hope that the earth would continue to yield more fortunes to those who sought it.

As the train began its deceleration into the depot at Washington and F Street, Sara took a much closer look at the city that she had chosen to call home. The V & T Train Depot lay at the extreme southern point of the town, so most of the places in which she would be able to find suitable work and lodging was farther north in the town proper. Just as the train entered the town, she could easily spot a mine which was identified as the Chollar Mine. She didn't have an inkling of an idea how much silver and gold this mine had produced during its day, but knowing how well-established it looked, it must have been a tremendous amount of wealth. There were what appeared to be some boarding houses and what looked like a hotel. She also spotted a school which, according to the sign on the building was the Fourth Ward School. There were a couple of government buildings, including the county sheriff office and a post office building. Finally, there stood an impressive mansion near the depot as well. It might be difficult for her, but in this town of nearly 6,500 souls she should be able to find a suitable place to live and work.

As Sara waited at the V & T Rail Depot for the train to unload all cargo and luggage, and while she sat on the bench near the baggage claim area, she marveled at what was going to be her new home. Here it was nearly 11:00 o'clock on this mid-July morning and by the thermometer gauge on the wall, Sara could see that it was nearing 74 degrees, a far cry less than the inferno she was told by well-meaning folks back in Bensenville who were trying to warn her of the oppressive heat 'out West.' What they all failed to consider was that Virginia City was at an elevation of 6,200 feet which did tend to have a pleasant cooling effect on the region.

As she sat patiently waiting for her trunk to be placed in the claim area, she was able to look out to see just what type of place she would be calling home. Gone were the brick paving and buildings of Reno; street lighting was also non-existent, and she could see that a vast majority of businesses, at least in this part of Virginia City, were saloons. She supposed that there would always be men who would devise some method of relieving others of their hard-earned wages. Back east it may have been through excessively high rents and union dues, but out here money exchanged hands in the saloons and brothels. It was said that more wealth was made in either supplying the miners' stake, or in satisfying their loneliness.

Sara did see that there were a handful of more desirable places in which she might find work. She caught a glimpse of a few eateries and some mercantile stores. With all the experience she had working in her parent's Emporium, she hoped she might find work in one of these types of establishments.

Suddenly, Sara spotted a young man who appeared to look very much like the young Mr. Sander whom she encountered in Reno the previous evening. He and another young man were making their way through the depot towards where she and Jesse were sitting. Of course, he was much more in control of himself today, although seeing the look on his face and the sallowness of his face, she could very well see that his exploits from the day before were not without cost. Frankly, he was for the most part, disheveled and out of sorts. It was fortunate for him that he had someone with him to keep him on a steady gate as he tried to maneuver towards what seemed to be his awaiting carriage.

As the two young men, both probably just short of 25 years old, passed Sara, the one whom she remembered was called Phil, glanced toward her. With a stop so sudden that it nearly bowled over the group of people following behind him, Mr. Sanders leered at Sara in such a manner that she began to feel extremely uncomfortable. If this was Phil Sanders sober, she much preferred to deal with the drunken version.

"I know you, don't I," he spoke to her in a repulsive manner.

"No sir, I don't believe so," she responded.

"No, we've met. Was it back in Kansas?"

"Sir, I've never been there. You are sorely mistaken, and I really need to be lookin' for my luggage," she stated as she picked up Jesse and headed toward the baggage claim area.

"Come on now, Phil!" his companion stated, "Your dad has sent the driver for you. You must make haste unless you want another lecture from the old man. You know how he gets."

Reluctantly, Phil turned back towards the waiting carriage, but as the two men made their way on towards the exit, he looked back to catch another glimpse of the young woman who had piqued his interest. He calmly reached up with his right hand to the brim of his derby in a gesture that seemed too familiar.

Sara must have felt the eyes of the young, apparently well-to-do rogue who apparently was arriving from Kansas City. Glancing back towards where the encountered had just occurred, she caught a glimpse of him as he leered at her in a most uncomfortable manner.

This encounter, along with a thousand other thoughts, ransacked Sara's mind and made her feel somewhat unsettled as she claimed her trunk and the few other things that she had brought with her from Bensenville. She was truly on her own now and would have learn quickly how to maneuver the chance meetings she would encounter with people like the young Phil Sanders. She could easily be a target, or she could learn how to fend for herself if she were to survive. She still had nearly $75 of the money the good people of her church back home had collected for her. She had to make certain that she prioritized things properly if she and Jesse were going to make it out here in Virginia City. She could end up like many of the other single girls and young women who had nothing else to turn to but selling themselves, but she was bound and determined that, with what she had learned back in Illinois, and her faith in God, she would not fall prey to the pitfalls that were nearly all around her.

Things were not quite what Sara was hoping for by the end of the summer of 1895. She had been surviving with her young baby son Jesse, but it seemed like she was reaching the end of her hopes. The money that she had received from her fellow parishioners back in Bensenville was completely exhausted by August. Not many people were eager to take in a boarder with a child so young. Most of the time, Sara and Jesse were able to find enough to eat from the cooks in the many eateries along C and D Street. Most of the workers in these cafes and saloons took pity on the young woman with the baby, as she was becoming known. Sometimes, a merchant would allow her to stay in a storage room in exchange for cleaning floors or washing dishes. Homelessness was not really a romantic idea to Sara, but through the waning summer and early fall, Sara and Jesse Harlin were becoming known and protected by many of the town's merchants.

It did not take long after arriving in Virginia City for Sara to begin thinking about finding a place to worship. It also did not take long for her to find out that there were but two places of worship in town; those two places were a catholic church called Saint Mary's in the Mountains on South E Street, and if you were not catholic, so far, the only other alternative was St. Paul's Episcopal Church a block over on South F Street. Since she had never really had any experience with Roman Catholicism or the Catholic Church, Sara decided very early that the best thing for the time being was to start attending services at the Episcopal church. Even though it wasn't the exact same thing as the Catholic faith, she still found it hard to become totally comfortable with the method of worship there.

But all of this was soon to change, and Sara would very quickly find something that would excite her longing to be an effective woman of God in the community and make a difference where she really felt she could. By the beginning of fall, 1895, Sara found herself a job working at the eatery called the Delta Café, which served the miners and travelers of the Comstock mines in the area. There were not too many establishments in Virginia City that were not brothels or Saloons, such as the Bucket of Blood Saloon, but the Delta Saloon, just down the street from the Bucket had established a more reputable kitchen to sell breakfast, lunch, and dinner. So many people passed through Virginia City that there was a dire need for hard working staff to man the city's food outlets. Sara was a hard worker and was soon working enough hours to afford a small room for Jesse and herself.

A group of nuns from the Sisters of Charity, which came out of the organization of Saint Vincent de Paul of San Francisco, had been established in Virginia City since a year before the end of the Civil War, meeting the special needs of the mining communities in the West. Besides the school, orphanage, and hospital that the nuns of the Sisters of Charity ran, they also provided care for pre-schooled aged children of working women. Sara was able to work and be assured that Jesse would be well kept while she was doing so. This was more than assuring for her as she was trying to carve a place for herself and her little boy in Virginia City.

It was at the Café where she worked that Sara overheard a conversation between two couples as they ate their lunch. Many things can be called pivotal points in a person's life, and some of those points can have a profound effect on the future of the person. This conversation she heard was just one of those times.

She knew right from the start, when these four came in to sit down for their meal, that they were Christians. The first thing they made sure they did when their food came to the table was to offer thanksgiving to God for the meal. In the couple of months that she had been working here the Delta Café this was the first time she had seen anyone take the time to ask the Lord's blessing on their food. Sara wanted to make every effort to be as helpful as she could for the two couples at this table. Being around fellow brothers and sisters in the faith always lifted her spirits up, especially when they were unafraid and unashamed to show that they served the Lord.

As she continued to stop by the table, asking if she could get anything or do any service that would make their meal more enjoyable, she was able to pick up some bits and pieces of their conversation that caused Sara's excitement levels to skyrocket.

"Sam, from all I'm hearing from the people I talk to, God's hand is all over this. We have before us a 'field ripe unto the harvest.' I know that there are two well-attended churches here, Sam, but Virginia City is ripe for an evangelical thrust into the area," George Kingly said as was cutting into his well-done steak dinner.

"I'm not sure, George. Have you taken a look around? Have you seen what we would be dealing with? George, I think there are more saloons and brothels here in Virginia City than there are dogs, and there isn't a shortage of those either!"

"Which makes it all the more important that we begin our work here as soon as we can. Don't you see Sam. Can't you feel the need here for the Lord's hand among these men?"

"I certainly see the need, George. I just know that this isn't Dallas. Why this isn't even Reno, for crying out loud! Are you sure you want to try to risk living here so far away from everything you're familiar with? What about you, Emily? Are you okay with coming here and starting a church here at the end of the world?"

"Sam," replied Emily Dawkes, George's wife, "I know that we have been told by Jesus Himself to go into all parts of the world with the gospel. I recollect that when our Lord said 'Go ye into the uttermost parts o' the world,' well, I take it He did mean we should be just lookin' for what's familiar."

"Yes, but ..."

"There's not a 'but' about it, Sam. We are church planters, and this town needs a church planted. As I see it, this is simple math; one plus one, and we are the two that God is called to come here to do it."

"Sam, both Emily and I have prayed hard about this. We are sure that this is where God wants us to labor for Him," interjected George.

"Alright, George. You both sound sure that this is God's will. I don't see how I there will be any problem convincing the rest of the elders back at Dallas First Baptist to back your mission here completely."

"To tell you the truth Sam, with or without the approval back home, we know this is God's will. This is where we are going to build another congregation."

"I'm glad to hear that, George. This is the kind of commitment that you need to do a work as big as you are about to do. Mary and I will head back tomorrow, and in the meanwhile, well, you should just follow the leadership of God."

Sara had cleared the plates off the adjacent table and was able to overhear the discussion between the two couples there. She headed back to the kitchen with her load of dirty dishes, and her mind full of exciting thoughts. Isn't this just the kind of thing she had done with the immigrant workers in Chicago along with the Steven and Joan Merra? Wouldn't this be something that she might be able to help with? She just knew that she had to connect with this couple who were trying to start a new church here in Virginia City. What were their names? She recalled the man being called George.

Knowing that she could not let the couple get away from here without contacting them, Sara set the dishes down in the back room to be washed and set out to use again, and then hurried out to see if they were still there at the table. To her dismay, all four of the people at the table were gone. She could not believe that she was missing this opportunity to serve the Lord again in the way that she was so comfortable doing.

As she approached the table to clear it off, she looked up just in time to spot that young man, Phil Sanders, coming into the café. And she also noticed that he spotted her too. She did not know why, but she just did not feel comfortable with the man. To her, it just seemed that his attention towards her made her feel somewhat uncomfortable. He hadn't taken his eyes off her and now he was making a point of veering away from the table he had originally chosen in order to seat himself in the section she was working in that morning.

"Well, we meet again," he said to Sara as he seated himself at the table she had just cleared.

Trying to be polite, Sara answered, "Sorry sir, do I know you?"

"Oh, I am certain you know exactly who I am. We have met. I would never forget a face as lovely as yours, Miss, …"

"If we have met, sir, why do you not recollect my name?"

"It's no matter. There are a lot of people I meet who I can never recall their names. Fortunately, I really don't need to remember other people's names. They only need to remember mine – Phil Sanders."

"And why's it so important to remember your name, Mr. Sanders?"

"I'm going to overlook your ignorance to the fact of who the Sanders are in this town. I understand that newcomers here don't know who anyone is here in the Comstock region, but if you want to last very long in this town, you've got to know who the Sanders family is. Most everyone who does business in this town does so with the help of my father. If anyone wants to set up any kind of operation here in Virginia City, well, I guess you might say that they have to make sure the Sanders family is okay with it," Phil Sanders stated as a matter of trying to impress Sara with his own self-importance.

Sara fully understood the meaning of the young man's little introduction. She knew that he looked at others as being beholding unto his family. The wealth of his family meant much to him, and he compared himself to others, not in terms of their worth as human beings but in terms of how he could best use them to his own advantage. She realized that the man she was looking at—this Phil Sanders—was just a younger version of her own father. It was clear to her that he would not stop until he got exactly what he wanted from other people. She wasn't too sure about what his father was like, but this she knew about Phil Sanders – he was a bully, just like her father and probably by now, her own brother.

"So, with whom do I have the pleasure of speaking?" Sanders asked, bringing Sara out of her reverie.

"Sara Harlin," was all she could say to him as she retreated into the kitchen.

A lot ran through her mind as she finished her shift at the Delta Café. She was excited about the prospect of connecting with the young couple who wanted to plant a new church group here in Virginia City. She wanted desperately to be a part of this new work, and she would do anything she could to find out the names of these two missionaries to the Comstock Mining region.

Also, on her mind was this Phil Sanders. He seemed to be one who would not stop until he got exactly what he was after. She had the uncomfortable feeling that she was what he was after. Why this was happening she could not understand. It seemed like for every hope she was given, there was also a test to go along with it. She wanted to make a home here in Virginia City and maybe even work with this couple who were trying to set up a new church for the miners; but this Sanders could, and probably would be an obstacle before her that would test her faith and her courage.

All Sara knew was that she would need to stay close to Jesus and follow His leading in her life. She had left everything to make a home for the baby she now thought of as her own. She was trying to find a place where she and Jesse would be accepted, and now she saw that here was yet again another challenge. But, here was also an opportunity to serve God. She was going to make the most of it. This she knew in her heart. She was going to stay strong in her faith and serve the Lord. She knew that God would be faithful to her.

Chapter Eight

It did not take long for Sara to find out about the new church that was being established by the couple named George and Emily Dawkes. Handbills were being circulated and posted all about the town at every business that might attract miners and other workers. The missionary couple also found an older, vacated building that once housed a saloon. The customary comments all through the established church community was that certainly the Lord would not be using a building that once was used to sell the 'demon rum' as a place to hold services for Him. Surely this would be a cursed place that would fall by the wayside, and the people who were attracted to such places to worship the Lord would necessarily clean up their lives before they could even think of attending a well-respected place of worship. Surely, anyone would be able to see this!

But George Dawkes and his wife Emily saw things differently, and they knew that they were called to this part of the country to do a different kind of work than what everyone expected. They really didn't see anywhere in the Word of God where Jesus came to live and die for a building. They knew that the church was not the building but rather, it was the gathered ones, the people, who made up the 'Bride of Christ.' They were not trying to establish a holy building; they wanted to help people see that they could be a holy community of believers, no matter who they were, as long as they were seeking the will of God in all they did. The building was surely important insofar as it was a tool to use for believers and followers of Christ to know God's will and grow in their faith.

It did not matter to Sara that this new church was meeting in an abandoned saloon. To her, if God would send His Son, the King of all kings, to be born in a stable, then a building that once sold liquor could be cleaned up and used as a new kind of stable. A new kind of wine could be served up in this building.

By the beginning of December 1895, Sara and a steadily growing fellowship of believers met as a new church in Virginia City. Most of these people who began attending this new church were the outliers of the town. Miners who had found faith in God, the women who formerly worked in the brothels and saloons, and some of the men who worked on the Virginia and Truckee Railroad were often seen attending services and even staying to talk with the more 'respectable' crowd. These so-called down-and-outers were plentiful in the city, and they made up a substantial portion of this new church group. But there were also a few who attended that were, in most circles, considered to be the best of society. These consisted of a few merchants, some of the people who worked in what could be considered 'good' jobs, and a few who attended were even some of the teachers of the Fourth Ward School.

There was one older couple that had grown particularly fond of Sara and the young boy Jesse since she had become involved in the new fellowship of believers. John Cormer and his wife Betty had been successful merchants in Virginia City since 1891 when they moved there from Boston. They had lost their only daughter, a fifteen-year-old, blond haired and blue-eyed girl who had died from the outbreak of Russian Flu in 1889. Trying as hard as they could to continue managing their hardware store back east, they just could not continue living somewhere that always reminded them of their dear Sadie. So, after much prayer and soul-searching, the middle-aged couple sold out their store and home in Boston, said their farewells to friends and acquaintances, and migrated west, opening a thriving mercantile store in Virginia City.

Their store, which they opened in the fall of 1891, served the needs of the miners who went into the surrounding area to set up claims and search for their 'pot of gold.' Since opening the store, John and Betty Cormer had built up one of the more successful enterprises in the area. Their business thrived as they served the needs of miners, and they also served the Lord.

It was not so much that the Cormers needed another employee that caused them to take in Sara and Jesse to work in the store and to live with them in their home, but it was also the uncanny similarity that Sara shared with their dear Sadie. Not only did the two girls share similar physical traits, but they also were very much alike in terms of their dispositions. It was just so amazing to both John and Betty how the Lord had filled a missing part of their life by providing a surrogate daughter, and as a bonus, a young boy who they could dote on as a grandson of sorts.

Sara was quite happy to be seen and treated as a daughter by this middle-aged couple. She felt that she had found the real parents that she had never had before; parents who loved her and accepted her son Jesse. Parents who were not filled with fear and hate but were accepting of others regardless of their shortcomings. So, Sara felt welcomed, and she felt like she had a home now. All was well with her now in the closing months of 1895.

Sara found security then, but there was still a conflict beginning to brew in her life. She could see it building, and it was as if a storm was threatening to break, and she could do nothing to stop it.

Phil Sanders was not the type of man to take no for an answer. He would not accept denial from Sara. After leaving her work at the Delta Café to live with and work for the Cormers in their mercantile, it did not take long for Sanders to find her. One crisply cold morning in December three young men along with Phil Sanders entered the store. Sara spotted Phil and did her best to remain out of his sight. There was just something about the man that Sara found distasteful, and she felt that it would be better to remain out of sight and mind rather than allow him to know that she was still around.

As the four young men moved from isle to isle in the store, Sara did her best to avoid being seen by Sanders. But try as she might, it was impossible for her to remain hidden from him for long. As she stood at the end of one of the isles, thinking she had avoided being spotted by him, she repeated her steps back to the isle that she thought the four young men had vacated. But as she did so, in her hurry to hide from Sanders, she nearly ran squarely into him. It seemed that he had separated from the other three men and backtracked down the very same isle that Sara was trying to make her escape.

"Why, Miss Harlin, isn't it?" queried Phil Sanders, as Sara stepped back from their collision.

"Yes, Mr. …," she hesitantly answered, not wanting Sanders to know that she knew his name.

"Sanders. But please, call me Phil. That's what I like my friends to call me."

"Yes, Mr. Sanders. How may I help you then?"

"Oh, there's a lot of ways you can help me now, Sara. That was the name you used when we saw each other at the café wasn't it?"

"Yes, that is my name, but I hardly think it's appropriate for those who are only acquaintances to be on first-name terms with each other, Mr. Sanders."

"Well, I'd like to try to change that, uhm, ... Miss Harlin. I'd like to think that we could be more than just friends. I'm thinking that maybe it would be awful nice of you to allow me to take you to a fine meal here in town tonight. What do you say about that?"

Trying to be as courteous as she could and not cause a scene there at work, she responded, "I think that we should probably leave things as they are, ... Mr. Sanders"

With that Sara quickly walked off, but Sanders called out so that nearly everyone in the store could hear, "We'll see about that, Miss Harlin! Just remember, I don't give up so easily, and I always get what I'm after!"

At that, Sara froze in her steps toward the sanctuary of the backroom, turned and was about to give a retort, but she thought better of it and decided her first instinct was right. She turned back towards the back workroom and hurried out of Sander's field of view so that, hopefully, he would accept this rejection gracefully.

As Sara was standing in a vacant spot near some merchandise that needed to be inventoried before placing out for sale, Joyce, a fellow employee, came into the stockroom to see if she was okay.

"Sara," Joyce called out, "are you okay?"

Trying to control her mixed emotions of fear and anger, Sara answer, "yes, I'm fine. I just had ta, get somewhere away from that man."

"I'm so sorry," Joyce responded. "I know the man you were talking to there. Sara, you were right to get back here away from him, and if you can do it, you need to stay away from that man. He usually doesn't stop till he gets what he's after!"

"Joyce, I'm not something anyone can be after."

"I know, Sara. I'm just warning you though. You need to stay away from him, Sara. He's not good."

"Thanks, Joyce. I'll do my best."

Things continued as they had for Sara and Jesse. Christmas came and went, another New Year was rung in, and now it was nearing mid-February 1896. The whole country, including the residents of Virginia City, were surprised about the admission of the forty-fifth state into the United States. For the past fifty years the people of Utah tried to be accepted into the Union, but one thing prevented the acceptance by the United States of a predominantly Mormon state – the practice of plural marriage. Knowing that to continue to hold on to this ideology would probably lead to the eminent destruction of their way of life, the leaders of their faith had been meeting for several years to address this issue. Finally, in 1890, the Mormon Manifesto was issued, and the doctrine of polygamy was denounced by the Mormon faith. Now, within five years, the people in Utah were accepted by the United States and early in January the territory became a state.

To the south of Nevada, a conflict was brewing everyone was calling the Yaqui Uprising. This seemed to be more of an issue concerning the Mexican government, so most of those in Virginia City only mentioned it in passing. It seemed to be something that was held as nothing more than 'small talk.' It was the kind of talk that most people carry on when the same way they talk about the weather.

For most of the people in Virginia City, and the rest of Nevada as well, the biggest talking point and issue that held their attention was the upcoming Presidential election. Nearly all of the people of the states in the Rocky Mountain region, including Nevada, were strong supporters of William Jennings Bryant, a strong advocate for replacing the gold standard of money with a silver standard. The whole issue in this election was all about the conflict between gold and silver. Most of the farmers in the west had been hit hard by the depression since 1893, and they felt that if the money could be backed mostly by silver rather than gold, then the nation could pull out of the hard economic times. Nevada, being predominantly a silver producing state, naturally backed Bryant for the Presidency against the Republican candidate, William McKinley.

To Sara, all of these things meant very little. A new interest had been sparked in her life and now it was kindled into a flame. One day after the first of the year a mountain of a man, Sam Horne, who everyone called "Bull," had entered the store and also entered her life.

Sam fit his moniker "Bull" to a tee. When Sara first saw him as he entered the store, the first thing she noticed was how he had to duck his head as he entered the store. His six foot seven, three-hundred-and-fifty-pound frame had collided with so many door frames that he had made it a habit of entering a room by ducking his head and turning to one side so that neither his head nor his shoulders would hit the door jams. Once a person met Sam, what impressed them more than his size was his gentle character. Sam was truly a big man with even a bigger heart. Sara could see right away, as Sam removed his hat and placed it on the hat rack at the entrance of the store, and then as he helped others to reach things on the top shelves, they would not normally be able to reach, she could see that he had a servant's heart. He did not see his size as a means to intimidate, but rather as a way to protect and defend the helpless.

What really endeared him to Sara was how truly kind and gentle he was. As was common with nearly all the miners, Sam also needed to stock up on supplies for the upcoming season in the fields. Things had to be purchased to meet the needs for the spring and summer, and Sam was there nearly every day to accrue all that he would need. Sara was finding that she was attracted to Sam and made a point of helping him find all that he needed. Of course, Sam knew exactly where everything he needed was located in the store, but he did not hesitate to seek Sara's assistance whenever possible. Their conversations began to become centered around more personal issues each time he visited the store for supplies.

Soon, Sara was beginning to learn all about Sam, or "Bull" as most of the other men called him. For instance, she found out that, unlike most of the miners who really had no plans for the wealth they would gather, Sam Horne had a goal for the wealth he would pull out of the ground. He wanted to eventually take that money, move to the San Juaquin Valley in California, buy a few hundred acres of prime farmland, and build a home and future for himself and whomever he would eventually marry.

At first, Sam's attempts to introduce himself to Sara were completely awkward at best. It took this mountain of a man several daily visits to the store before he could even work up the courage to begin a simple conversation with her. Day after day, he would come into the store fully intending to break the ice with Sara, only to find that he could not bridge the gulf between an occasional tip of the hat to her and a full-fledged conversation. But on one bright, crisp March morning, he threw all caution aside, and standing in the aisle where the Levi dungarees were stocked, he timorously asked Sara, "Pardon me ma'am! Can you assist me?"

"Why I surely can, sir. How may I be of assistance?" she returned, happy that he had finally broken the ice.

Sam had finally taken a giant step in making some sort of contact with the young woman, but he hadn't planned much beyond just saying something to her. He had bridged the gap, but now he had to follow through. Standing there amid the dungarees, he asked furtively, "Where might I find your work clothes for sale?"

All Sara could do, in response to his question, was to look to each side of Sam with a little smile of satisfaction that at least they he had made contact with her.

Sarah and Jesse had now found more permanent living quarters at the Capitol Lodging House run by Rose Sissa. This lodging facility was at one time a hotel run by Rose's husband Eugene, but by 1870, the local newspaper The Territorial Enterprise, where a young Samuel Clemens worked and became known by his more familiar name, Mark Twain advertised this as one of the finest lodging facilities in the city. But by the time Sara and Jesse arrived in Virginia City, Mrs. Sissa had taken control of the lodging establishment and turned it into a boarding house. Sara was quite a bit younger than the other women who were living in the home, but they took her in without question and accepted this young unmarried mother of an infant. Everyone just assumed that Sara was at one time married, but lost her husband in the mines, which occasionally did happen.

This time saw the beginning of a special friendship between Sara Harlin and Samuel Horne. When folks in town saw the three together – Sara, Sam, and Jesse (for Sara would never think of courting a man who would not accept her son) – they would smile with inward delight at the trio. There had not been a more odd-looking ensemble on the streets of Virginia City in as long as anyone could remember. It was particularly poignant when they saw the giant of a man gently carrying the small, young boy in his arms. Sam was known for both his size and his explosive anger, especially when he witnessed what he perceived to be injustice done towards the helpless.

Sara had witnessed this herself when she was at work one morning. Looking out the window of the store, she spotted a woman running away as if being chased by a demon, and a young man caught in the grip of a bear hug by Sam. She could see that the young man was struggling just to keep from passing out as eventually having his upper arms and chest crushed by the giant of a man. She knew that something was amiss as she rushed out of the store to intervene and hopefully keep Sam from doing something that he and everyone else would regret. It was all that she could do to bring Sam back to some presence of mind so that she could coax him into letting the man go before killing him, but finally Sam released him. The man collapsed at their feet, and Sara grabbed Sam and steered him away from the victim of his anger and back into the store, quite possibly saving the man's life.

"Sam, what on earth are you doing? You nearly killed that man out there!"

She could see that Sam was struggling with his anger, trying to calm himself down so that he could respond to Sara. Within ten minutes his glazed and fixed expression of hate and anger began to subside, and Sam began to be fully aware of his surroundings.

Seeing that he was back to some form of calm, Sara repeated, "What happened Sam? What set you off so?"

"Is she okay, Sara?"

"Is who okay? Sam, are you aware that you nearly killed a man out there this morning?"

At that moment, a sheriff's deputy entered the store, and made his way to where Sara was trying to calm her friend.

"Sam Horne! What are we going to do with you? Mr. Horne, you nearly killed Mr. Chesterton today!" the deputy stated.

Sara responded to the deputy's query, "Deputy Reeves, Sam was trying to help someone out there. He'd never hurt anyone, lessin' there was good reason for it!"

"Yes, I've talked to both the woman and the man that Sam nearly destroyed out there. Seems like that man may have needed to be stopped from harassing her, but it doesn't seem that what he did warranted nearly being killed by a 'good Samaritan' as what nearly happened this morning."

"You know I'd never meant to kill the man, deputy. I was only trying to stop him from causing that lady any harm. Is she okay?"

"She's somewhat shook from everything that happened, but she's going to be fine. I'm not so sure about Chesterton though. I'm pretty sure that he's got to deal with a few broken ribs."

"So, Deputy, are you takin' me in?"

"By rights I should, Sam. But seein' that Chesterton more than likely needed to be reminded that the women of Virginia City are not his playthings, and since he's probably going to think twice before trying to bully his way around others. I know that he's good friends with Sanders and his son, Phil, but that don't give him rights to get whatever he wants."

Sara was troubled somewhat by the events that had occurred. She was torn by Sam's actions and his inability to control his temper. Looking at Sam now, she saw that he was also a deeply troubled man. Sara knew of only one solution to this deep-seated anger that she saw that morning. She knew of only one way to truly change a person from the inside out, and she was determined that she would be the one who would help Sam overcome this and any other underlying conditions. There was truly a good man there, and she was determined to introduce him to the one who could unleash that goodness.

Sam stared at the words on the page of the new bible that Pastor Dawkes had given him. George Dawkes had been helping Sam learn more about this faith that Sara had been trying to introduce him to. It wasn't that Sam had not ever attended church in the past, but this was the first time that anyone from a congregation, let alone a pastor, had spent so much time trying to teach him about this Jesus from the past. Oh, he had known what seemed like his whole life about Christmas and Easter, but it all seemed so very strange to Sam. Things that he read from the Bible such as turning your cheek and forgiving your enemies; well, it all seemed so foreign to this mountain of a man. Bull Horne was never one to let others know that he would not be pushed around. He would fight for what he thought was right and, need be he would defend anyone he felt close to, even if it meant that someone would have to die.

This would all play a major role in the transformation of Sam Horne, in a most unexpected way. It was not long before his whole world was turned upside down. A brand-new person would soon be living in Virginia City, and it would all come about, it a most auspicious manner.

"Land's sake, Sara! You best get on home now," Betty Cormer called out to Sara, who was busy working in the stock room.

"Are you sure, Mrs. Cormer?" Sara replied. "I can stay a while longer and help."

"No dear, you go on now and get some dinner and a good rest tonight."

"If you're sure. It would be nice to spend some time playin' with Jesse tonight 'fore he falls asleep."

With that exchange, Sara took leave of the mercantile store, and began walking towards the Smithson's home where Jesse had been babysat for several weeks now.

The streetlights that had been recently upgraded were lit, and a darkness was settling in around Sara as she anxiously made her way to retrieve her son from the Smithson's home. Sara was not fond of this time of day, as some of the rougher groups of people were beginning to assemble on the streets of Virginia City. To Sara, the walk home was filled with danger from the unknown elements of the city.

As she made her way around the first turn and headed into a darker, less protected, portion of the town, a sinister figure was looming in the deepening shadows behind Sara. Eyeing the young woman, and keeping a few hundred feet distance behind her, Phil Sanders was also making his way towards the Smithson home. But he didn't plan to follower Sara all the way there. He knew just exactly where he would make his move. He felt that she had disrespected him beyond anything he was able to endure. How dare she spurn his attempts at what he called cordiality. After all, his family was one of the most respected in this community, and she had no right to treat him in this manner. At least that is what he had convinced himself. To Phil Sanders, this upstart little two-bit 'better-than-all' Sunday School girl would have to learn a lesson in life. You don't deny the desires of a member of his family. That's the unspoken rule and the law by which he lived.

'Tonight, is the night,' he thought to himself, 'and she's going to get what she deserves,'

Also headed towards where Sara was quickly walking was Sam. His mind was filled with more questions about his struggles to understand her faith. He hoped that she might be at home so that she could answer some of the questions.

Minute by minute, and second by second, the trio was converging on one point just a block away from the Smithson's home. Sara made the final turn onto the street on which their home was located, only to be suddenly grabbed from behind by Sanders. He grasped her by the waist with one hand, put his other hand over her mouth to conceal any screaming she might emit, and pulled her into the darker recesses of the narrow street. Every attempt by Sara to free herself from the grasp of Sanders only caused his vice-like hold to tighten. She felt as helpless as a two-year-old.

Phil Sanders might have succeeded in his heinous attack on the young woman, but providence was abundantly helping her. Sam saw the attack take place from its inception, and he was quick to respond. Within less than ten seconds, he raced to Sara's help, loosening the grip of her assailant, and quickly separating him from the one he had grown so close to.

The problem though, was that Sam's righteous anger was not assuaged by just removing Sara for eminent danger. Bull Horne saw red, and when he did there was no stopping him. He applied the force of his anger onto the face and upper body of Sanders. He could not be stopped from his attacks on the smaller man. Blow upon blow was showered upon Sanders until he was just a limp ragdoll man who presented no further threat to Sara, or to anyone else for that matter.

But still, Sam's rage continued. Had it not been for the intervention of three other men who were drawn to the fight, Phil Sanders would have been dead right then and there. But, the storm within Sam was sated, and peace was restored to the scene.

As the bystanders were attending to Sanders and administering rudimentary first aid, and as Sara was trying to assure Sam that she was alright, deputies showed up and began to question those who witnessed the events. None of those present were there to have seen Sanders initiate the attack on Sara, nor to have seen Sam coming to her defense.

Everyone but the three only showed up after the fact. There was no other course for the lawmen to take but to have Phil Sanders sent to the hospital for medical treatment; to have Sara released into the care of the Comers; and to arrest Sam Horne for causing severe injuries to Sanders.

Although being held in jail may have seemed to have been a miscarriage of justice, in the end it was just what was needed for both Sam and Sara. She was able to visit him on a regular basis, and the two became even closer to one another than before. For the first time in her life, Sara felt that God had led someone to her that showed her the love that she had been seeking for a long time.

But still, there was the big issue she knew stood between her and any further relationship she could establish with Sam. He was not born again. Yes, he was a sincerely good and well-meaning man, but he was still dead in his sins. Sara knew that she loved Sam, and she also knew that Sam loved her. But still, they were not equally yoked, and it was important to her that she would find a man who loved God more than he loved her.

Sam struggled with this as Sara continued to share the love of Christ with him. Was it not enough for her to know that he would not hesitate to defend her to the point of killing anyone who was a threat to her? Wasn't she aware that he would do the same for her son Jesse? How could she deny that he loved her?

Within a couple of weeks, Phil Sanders was recovering from the injuries of the fight. His friends tried to convince him that he should press charges against Sam. But Sanders was, if not anything else, a young man who could see when things had gotten out of hand, and he had lost what he always sought for in every situation - control. Taking Sam to court, and possibly prison, was not going to accomplish anything. Besides, he really wasn't that attracted to this independent young woman. He didn't see any real advantage to staking his claim with her, and, truth be told, he knew that that claim would probably not amount to the effort he had to put forth. Had he let his own pride drive him to the point of almost driving himself to the point of doing something no different than the riffraff he always looked down upon would do. To Sanders, the better course would be to just bide his time and wait for the most opportune moment to get even. Besides, Sara came with too much baggage - having a little boy to take care of - and he didn't need any more responsibilities in his life.

Sam had been released from jail for about a week or so when Sara went to his cabin to see if he was doing okay. It was quite a surprise, after finding him sitting behind his house with his bible open, to find him with tears running down his cheeks. She wondered what could have caused him such distress that he would be crying.

"Sam," she said as she walked upon the back step of his home. "Are you okay?

"I have been such a fool, Sara!"

"Whatever do you mean?"

Holding up the bible, Sam looked at her and said, "All this time, Sara. All this time I thought it was about how everyone else is the problem. To me, everyone else was in the wrong. I just thought that I was doing the right thing by doing what I did, and that should be enough to be one of Christ's."

"Sam, what are you saying?"

"I've read what Jesus said, Sara. It ain't about anyone else! It's not what everyone else has to do, Sara. I must forgive them, Sara. Jesus said so. I've got to learn that to be a child of God, I've got to trust Jesus, and forgive as much in others as Jesus forgave in me."

"Oh, Sam. That's right!"

"Sara, I can't hate anymore. I have to learn to forgive. Sara, I want to belong to Jesus. Will you help me? Will you show me how to be saved?"

"Of course, I will," she replied as she looked up to the heavens in thanksgiving.

Chapter Nine

Had he been so blind that he couldn't see how wrong he had been? Yes, a lot of things had changed in the short amount of time since Sam became a Christian. It seemed as if the anger that often would emerge as he dealt with other people, just simply never found the fuel needed to erupt into its usual fury. It wasn't that Sam was not still faced by the same issues has before, but now his priorities were all set in a different direction. Oh, the desire to succeed as he worked in the mines was still there, but now it was there for a different reason. What used to be a desire to strike paydirt so that he could quickly purchase that farm he had dreamed of was being slowly, but surely modified to being more and more patient. The Lord's timing was becoming more and more important to Sam.

One of the most notable changes that his many coworkers began to take note of was Sam's much more gentle spirit. He seemed to have developed a longer fuse when it came to getting angry. The things that used to always send Sam into a rage now merely gave him pause for thought.

For many of his former so-called friends, the changes taking place in the big man were somewhat disappointing and disconcerting. There was nothing that they used to find more entertaining than to see Sam become enraged at the least provocation. Now, their childish form of entertainment was quickly fading away. The more they tried to set him off in a fit of anger, the more and more they were disappointed. Surely, they thought, we can have another few laughs at Sam's expense. It would just mean having to find the right formula to ignite his emotions beyond his control.

There were two factors working on Sam, bringing about this miraculous change. First, since this new year of 1896 had rolled around, his relationship with the Lord was blossoming. Oddly enough, the closer he was getting to Jesus, the more he wanted to read his bible; and the more he read his bible, the closer he got to God.

The second factor was even more than apparent this crisp morning in late March. The big man could be seen driving a small horse-drawn buggy down "C" Street, wearing his Sunday finery, trying the best way he could just to balance a small bundle of flowers in his hand, while trying to control steerage of his vehicle. He was an uncommonly strange sight, perched precariously on the buggy, all suited up, with a bowler hat adorning his head, and driving determinately towards Sara's lodging at the Capitol Lodging Home.

There was no shortage of taunting taking place by those other young men that he passed by as he drove his buggy to Rose Sissa's Capitol Lodging House. Several people called out to Sam making various comments. Some were just light-hearted teasing, while others tended to be a little more biting and insulting. But Sam seemed to be most determined in the task before him and paid very little attention to what was being yelled out to him.

Sara was all a fluster as she readied herself for upcoming evening with Sam. She was trying her hardest to get dressed while, at the same time, attending to her young son who was getting into everything since he began walking just a couple of months previously. It seemed that little Jesse was continually moving from one object of interest to another. He was definitely a curious young boy at a little more than 19 months old.

Thankfully, a knock of the door sounded as Sara was trying desperately to keep Jesse from pulling the young mother's basket of cosmetics and toiletry items from the small dressing table onto the floor. As Sara quickly saw to keeping the boy from making a total mess of everything, there was again a knock at the door and the familiar voice of Annabel Adams at the door. What a God send Mrs. Adams had been for Sara.

Annabel, or Anna, as she preferred her friends to call her, was a woman about the age of 45 or so who had had lost her husband and only son in a mining accident that took place a few months before Sara and Jesse had first arrived in Virginia City. It did not take very long for Anna to establish a friendship with Sara very soon after meeting her at Cormer's Mercantile Store where the young girl was working. It seemed to Anna that Sara would kind of fill the void left by the loss of her son, and Jesse would be a bonus – a grandson she lost all hope of ever having.

"I'm comin' Anna," Sara called out, making her way to the door.

The warm smile on Anna's face as she stood there at the open door had a soothing effect over Sara, as she was becoming more and more flustered.

Stepping into the little compartment, Anna said, "It seems your young gentleman caller is quite preoccupied, Sara. He's waiting for you down in the sitting room, but he sure in fact is havin' hisself a right hard time. If you was to ask me, I'd say he's got somethin' on that mind a' his."

"Oh Anna, I'm sure it's got somethin' ta do with somethin' he read in his Bible."

"I don't know. I reckon you're 'bout to find out sooner or later. You go on now. I'll take little Jesse to downstairs to my room, and when he gets back tonight, you can tell me all about what it is."

"Anna, I don't know what I'd do without you helpin' out with my boy."

"You just go on now. Jesse and me will have us a good ole' time, won't we, son?" Anna replied as she nudged Sara out of her own door.

Well, it was sure like Anna was trying to tell Sara. There was something huge consuming Sam's thoughts. All through dinner, he kept fidgeting with his coat pocket as if he were trying to find something there. At times, beads of perspiration began to form themselves upon his forehead.

Finally, unable to keep quiet, Sara said, "Sam, there is obviously something botherin' you. It seems that you are quite beside yourself. Is there anything you're meanin' to say?"

The look that crossed Sam's face was one of both relief and abject horror. He knew that he was not going to be able to keep his thoughts to himself much longer, and rather than try to be cool, calm, and collected, which was never his style, Sam just blurted out what was on his mind, "Sara, we need to get married!"

There. It was said and done. No going back now as Sam looked sheepishly into the stunned expression on the face of the young girl that he had fallen so much in love with. Everything within him wanted to pull the words out of the air, but what was said was now registering in the mind of Sara.

What was started could not be undone, so the big man continued to unload his thoughts, trying the best he could to make Sara understand.

"Sara, I love you more than you can ever know. If it weren't for you, my life would be incomplete. I love that young'un of yours too. I just know that the good Lord wants me to take you and Jesse as my family, to care for and protect for the rest o' my life. I'm completely out o' sorts when I'm away from you. I want us to be known, wherever we go, as Sam, Sara, and Jesse Horne. I will adopt your son and raise him as my own. Sara, please say you'll be mine!"

Sara was completely caught off guard. She also loved Sam and was hoping that someday they would become a family. Deep down inside she knew that this was God's will for her life, but there was one thing that made her hesitant to come right out and accept Sam's proposal. Sam had said that he would adopt Jesse, but that was her hang-up. She had never officially adopted him herself. When Soninka had died, there was never anything legally done to make him her own son. She had known that the courts would have just handed him over to some foundling where he would never have been given the love that she did.

What would Sam think of her? In reality, she was nothing more than a kidnapper even though no one other than her really cared what happened to baby Jesse. She could not stand it if Sam would stop respecting her or even start hating her for what she had done a little more than a year ago. She didn't know what she would do if Sam became disgusted and walked out of her life, and it was just then that she realized that she really did love this mountain of a man.

So, she knew right then and there that, if she really did love him, and she knew that she did, then she had to confess her secret to him. That is exactly what Sara did for the next few moments of time. But the scornful look she was expecting, and the horror that she knew Sam must have felt never materialized.

Sam's reply was straightforward, "Sara, everything you have just told me has only made me love you more than ever. You are such a strong, God-fearing woman. I could never see myself loving any other woman as much as I love you. You saved young Jesse from a life that I cannot imagine. It doesn't matter one wit to me whether he has my name or just keeps the one he's got. No one besides you and I have to even know what his name is. He is your son, and I want to help raise him to become a strong young man who will learn to love the Lord. I promise you Sara, you will never have to doubt my love for you and Jesse."

And it was done! They did not plan for a long engagement and a large wedding, but rather, they just prepared a small, intimate gathering of friends and church family to celebrate their nuptials.

Before the couple were married, they were able to find a small, older, two-bedroom home located at the east end of Sutton Street. This would be a good place to grow as a small family, and maybe save up for Sam's plan of purchasing land in the San Juaquin Valley in California. He still wanted to build a farm and raise a strong family.

The wedding occurred during the first week of July and was held at the modest chapel of the old Presbyterian Church on C Street. Sara's employers had good friends who were members of this church, and they were able to obtain the services of the pastor and the facilities for the wedding.

One lone figure stood outside the church as the two were joined. Old memories welled up, as Phillip Sander stood there with a malicious glare on his face. Ever since it was common knowledge that Sara and Sam were to be married, Sanders had done all that he could to financially ruin him. With all the strings his family could pull, and the control they exercised with the banks and money lenders, he had made it impossible for Sam to work in the major company mines. Oh, Sara could marry Horne, but she would be marrying a ton of hardship and he would see to that. Still, he wasn't done.

Chapter Ten

Yes—Sanders was not finished. There was payback that needed to be exacted. For that reason alone he would often make his way to the Horne home on Sutton Street just to formulate his plan. He continually asked himself how he could best get even with Sam Horne and his silly little family.

It had become an obsession for Phillip Sanders. What he did know was that he had been insulted, and he would not let any chance to destroy the Horne family get away from him. It gradually became apparent to him that the most satisfying and most efficient way to deal with Sam Horne was to force him to take his little family and move away from Virginia City. There was no better way to do that than to burn everything that Sam owned. He would bide his time, and when everyone was gone away, such as when they were attending some church service, he would burn the house and all its contents to the ground. Sanders felt this was fool-proof plan, and he would waste no time getting everything set into order. He would just have to watch the Horne family to see what their habits were and when he could successfully complete his plan.

John Slater had asked Sam if he could borrow his wagon on the Wednesday night prior to Christmas Day. Normally Sam, Sara, and Jesse would be heading off to the mid-week church services that were being held, but the week Jesse was a little bit ill, and the family would more than likely stay home that Wednesday evening.

Slater arrived at the Horne's home to get the wagon and drove the horses off into the dark night air. Ducking into the shadows two blocks away from the house was a sinister figure carrying an unlit torch and a full canister of kerosene. He stayed well hid, watching the wagon drive by.

He thought to himself, "Isn't that nice? The lovely couple is headed off to their holier-than-thou gathering. Little do they know what will be waiting for them when they return to what's left of their home.

As soon as the wagon had made the turn at the next corner, the man in the shadows resumed his journey towards the little rental house the Horne family lived in. He had to make sure that he would remain in the dark shadows to conceal his identity from any chance witnesses.

Before too long, Sanders spotted his objective. He thought it was strange that they would leave so many lamps lit in the house. There were at least two rooms that were still illuminated. He figured that they were probably in a hurry to get to their stupid little preaching and singing service and completely forgot to put out the lamps. Oh well, a little more fire would not hurt anything. As a matter of fact, it would be pretty much eaten up by the fire that he intended to start.

Slowly and quietly, he crept toward the back of the house to begin baptizing the house with the contents of the can of kerosene he held in his hand. Good thing the family doesn't own a dog or some other animal that would warn the neighbors of what he was up to. Once he had liberally doused the back of the house, he came back around and emptied the contents of the can in the front. He wanted the house to be fully involved in destruction before the fire wagons could get there to salvage anything. Everything must be destroyed.

Sam was pretty sure he had heard something just outside, but he couldn't quite make out what it was. He quietly slipped into the dark confines of the storage closet near the front door and retrieved his Winchester rifle.

"Sara, I need to check something outside. You stay here and keep Jesse safe," he called out to his wife.

"What on earth, Sam? Why are you takin' that gun with you?"

"Sara, just stay inside," Sam answered as he headed out the front door. After a cursory look to see if there was anyone out in the front, he decided to make his way around the house to the back. If anything was going on that should not be happening, it would more than likely be in the back, out of sight.

Sanders was pretty sure that he heard the front door to the house shut. He thought that he had better get around there and find out if any nosey neighbors might have discovered his presence.

Once he got back around to the front of the house, the only thing that Phil could see was an empty porch. Things looked just the same as they did a few minutes earlier when he had first arrived at the house.

"Better hurry up and get this done," he said to himself as he continued to splash the kerosene onto the wooden façade of the front of the house.

Once he had emptied the kerosene, Sanders retrieved the torch that he had left in the bushes, lit a match, and then ignited the torch. As he ran back up onto the porch, he accidentally knocked over a small table that was holding a ceramic vase of flowers that Sara had left out. It fell to the ground with a resounding crash that might attract the attention of the neighbors. Quickly, Phil set the burning end of the torch to the newly distributed kerosene and instantly the wood dry wood of the house and porch ignited.

Within a few moments the entire front of the structure was engulfed in flames which were quickly spreading around to the back of the house.

Sam could hear the crashing sound of what he knew was the vase that Sara had left out on the front porch. Thinking that it might have been upset and knocked over by a prowling cougar, Sam dashed back towards the front of the house.

Suddenly, a man carrying a lit torch appeared, running from the front of the house. Just at the same moment, the man with the torch realized that Sam had not been on that wagon that passed by him earlier. He also knew that there was no way Horne was going to let Sara go out to the church unaccompanied at night. It instantly dawned on Sanders that he had set fire to the house while the family were still at home. It was quite possible that he had committed more than arson. He very likely committed the murder of a young woman and two-year-old boy as well.

Both the front and the back of the house were enveloped in the flames from the fire. The dry wood of the home, along with the soaking it received from the kerosene, was enough to create an inferno.

Both Sam and Phil realized instantaneously that Sara and Jesse were inside the jaws of a growing fire that would soon consume everything in its way. Both men turned and ran towards the house hoping that they could get the two out before it was too late. Sam dropped the rifle and ran to the nearest window to try to get in to rescue his family. He knew exactly where his wife and son were so he ran to the window closest to the room they might be in if they had not yet moved from it.

Sanders had no idea what the interior layout of the house was, nor did he know exactly where Sara or Jesse might be. Nevertheless, he ran as fast as he could to the back door of the house which to him seemed to be the most logical thing to do.

Sam had made it into the totally engulfed house and very soon found his young wife, who was holding Jesse close to her body and trying to shield him as much as possible from the increasing heat and smoke. Thankfully, Sara had the great sense to bring Jesse down the stairs from where he was sleeping. It seemed to Sam that both of them were alright, but he knew he had to get them out of the ever-increasing flames and suffocating smoke.

Sam would surely deal with Sanders later, but right now he had to get his family to safety. As quickly as he could, Sam grabbed an unburned article of clothing and shielded Sara and Jesse in order to take them out through the window that he had entered through.

It was a harrowing experience for the three of them, but the Horne's were soon out and away from the house which by now was totally wrapped in flames. Neighbors were by now arriving and lending all the help they could, and someone had the sense to telephone the fire department, which by the sound of the clanging bell had sent out a fire wagon to render whatever help they could.

To the people gathered at the still-burning house, Sam seemed a little bit distracted. He seemed to be looking for someone particular. His gaze moved from person to person as if he was trying to find some long lost soul. Still, the little house that the Horne family called home continued to burn along with all the earthly possessions that they owned. There were sudden flare ups of the flames and from time-to-time small popping sounds emitted from the fire. It was obvious that there was not going to be anything salvaged from this disaster. The long-and-short of it was that Sam, Sara, and Jesse had lost everything in the world that they owned.

"Look Horne," said the stern-voiced sheriff of Storey County, "I need some answers, and I need them really quick."

The burned body of the one assumed to be Phillip Sanders was found when the firemen extinguished the flames, and the authorities could begin their investigation of the matter. Sam knew full-well that it was Sanders he saw standing there with the torch. He also knew that the fire would not have been so thoroughly destructive if it did not have help to take hold.

The remains were identified by the signate ring and one boot that was still intact which held the initials "P.S." stamped inside. Andrew Sanders, the father of Phillip, was completely grief-stricken.

He knew that his son was not perfect by any means, but he was still his son, and he loved him dearly.

Sam knew that Mr. Sanders was really a kind old man whose heart had been blinded by love for a son who he had always hoped would one day become a good person. But Mr. Sanders was blinded to the fact that Phil was just not a descent young man. Too many years of getting everything he ever wanted without putting any effort into acquiring it had taken root in Phil and until the night he died he felt that everyone was obligated to serve him.

Still, Sam could not bring himself to hurt the broken father of Phil Sanders. This was quite a quandary for Sam. Should he lie about what he knew of Phil's involvement in the fire? Lies never help anyone in the end, and usually just cause more pain than the brutal truth. Saying nothing when he knew what really happened would be the same as a lie. So, he couldn't just feign ignorance. But the truth would probably destroy a grief-filled father. What should he do?

The matter was taken out of Sam's hands though when his friend John Slater revealed eventually revealed to the sheriff what he had seen the night of the fire. It seems that either Phillip Sanders was not so good at hiding, or that Slater had some sort of sixth sense and could just feel the presence of another person. It was probably the first.

"It seemed odd to me at the time to see Sanders hiding in the shadows, thinking that he was some kind of invisible," stated Slater.

"So, just what did you see Phil Sanders doing?" asked the sheriff.

"Well, after I picked up the wagon from Sam, I drove off down the street. Before I could get to the end and make my turn, I caught someone, quick-like, hide in the shadows. As I passed him, I saw that it was Sanders, and I thought how strange it was that he was a' holding a torch and a can of something or other."

"Hmmm. Must have been a can of something to start the fire with," thought the sheriff out loud.

"Sheriff!" interjected Sam. "Does Mr. Sanders really need to know all of this, right now?"

"Well Sam, it might not serve any practical purpose right at the moment. But you do know that he will eventually need to be given the truth about his son."

"Thank you, Sheriff!"

"Alright Sam, but you listen to me. Don't go telling any stories about what happened. One day his father will be told the truth, and it won't help anything at all if Phil Sanders is labeled a hero."

Chapter Eleven

Another New Year's came and went, and a new year was born. The small family were doing the best that they could, though it was tough. Without the help of their church family and other friends, things were bleak at the very best. The one saving grace that the couple experienced was the mildness of the winter. That, at least, was comforting.

It was surprising how much stuff people give you when you are really in need, and the Horne family was just that – really in need. They had very little before the devastating fire, but in the aftermath of the disaster, it did not take long for it to sink in that they had absolutely nothing.

Sam and Sara cherished everything and anything that everybody gave them. Someone in their church even allowed the family to move into an old barn that they had on their property. Sara still worked, so they could at least feed their family. Sam did not have the steady income that he so desired, and that was beginning to fester within him. So it was that news began to circulate about a huge gold strike in Alaskan Territory.

Many people had some thought provoking terms for the acquisition of the Alaskan Territory from Russia back in late 1867. Some called it Johnson's Polar Bear Garden, after the President who was in office at the time. Other endearing terms were Walrussia, Russian Fairy Land, and most recently the purchase of the Alaskan Territory was referred to as Seward's Folly.

But many people began to question the supposition that it was indeed a mistake to buy the land from Russia. Everyone knew that it cost the taxpayers a hefty $7 million, but they also knew that at the size of the land gained to the United States, the cost was something like two cents per acre – a bargain in most people's minds.

It was especially satisfying to many people in the country when it was reported that a small group of four souls, namely George Carmack and his Tagish wife Shaaw Tláa, along with her brother Skookum Jim and his son Káa Goox, discovered gold in late August of 1896 on the Rabbit Creek, in the Klondike region of Alaska. It was not long before others made their way to the Klondike region and began to prove that the rumors of the discovery were, in fact, true. It was said that thousands of people, soon to be known as "stampeders," were making their way to the vast regions of the Yukon Territory.

Sara could feel the restlessness in Sam as the weeks after the fire began to pass. She knew that his inability to provide for Jesse and herself was taking its toll on the now brooding but quiet Sam Horne. He worked as much as he was able to, but in the weeks and months prior to his death, Phil Sanders had successfully had Sam blacklisted and non-hirable. Outwardly, to the members of their small Christian fellowship, Sam Horne exuded a kind and patient reserve. But on the inside, Sara could see the increasing rage beginning to surface. He would never display any anger towards Jesse or herself, but small, insignificant problems and situations seemed to propel him into a darker, more silent rage. He was becoming an unvented Dutch oven ready to explode.

Sara knew that the only remedy for any problems that her husband was dealing with would be to sit down and talk it out. Maybe, just maybe there was some things they could do together to ease the burdens that Sam was feeling.

After a very busy day at the mercantile store, Sara's mind was rehearsing how she would brooch the subject and get Sam to open up about whatever it was that was seeming to consume him more and more each passing day. As if right on cue, Sam entered the barn which had been converted into a small and very drafty home.

Knowing that it could not wait any longer, Sara spoke out, "Sam, I think it's time that we had a talk 'bout whatever it is botherin' you."

This opening by Sara was met with a very loud silence. She could see the frustration on his face, and she could also see the tears beginning to well up in his eyes. She had never seen her husband on the verge of breaking down, and she was a bit frightened. But she knew that now that the can was opened, there was nothing to do but empty its contents.

"Sam, something deep is botherin' you, and it must be gotten out."

"I know, Sara, I know!" Sam answered.

"Sam, you know how much I love you, and there is nothin' I would not do nor give up for you. What is it, Sam?"

"I'm not good, Sara. I feel like a total failure; to you, to Jesse, and especially to God. It's my one job, Sara, to see that you and Jesse are taken care of, but I've completely failed at that."

"Sam, I don't blame you for what that Phil Sanders has done to you."

"Sara, I don't want to blame God, but it's getting' harder and harder each day not to."

"Don't say things like that, Sam. God has been really good to us. You know that don't you, Sam?"

"Yes, I do know that, Sara. But sometimes it feels like no matter what I do, doors just keep getting' closed in my face."

"Well, Sam, I think we got to keep looking for other doors. Ones that are open." Sara responded encouragingly.

"Sara," Sam said with a new tone in his voice, "There is something that has been playing through my mind. I was just fearing it might be just another bad thought though."

"What is it, Sam? Tell me!"

"Well Sara, you know that I'm a miner, right?"

"Of course, Sam."

"Okay, well, no one is talkin' much about round here, but the silver's done been playing out now for some time. You know how things have been slowing down."

"Yeah, business has been dropping off quite a bit, and a lot of the miners we know have moved off to that Yukon Territory."

"Sara, that's what's been on my mind. I've been thinking a lot about it, but I've been hesitating to bring it up to you. I think I should be goin' up there too."

"You should be goin' up there? Wait a little minute mister. If you are going to go trapsing off to the gold fields, you are not leaving Jesse and me here alone."

"Sara, I know you love me, and I love you too, but I don't think that dragging my family to some place where its unbelievably cold and forsaken as that place up there is such a good idea. Sara, I hear that once it gets to October, the temperature can drop down to minus 58°, and that can last all the way up to the next June."

"Will, it looks to me like I would just need to double up on the long handles and bring along some nice heavy blankets. But Sam, I said that you are not leavin' me and Jesse here by ourselves."

"Sara, I do want to at least try up there in order to earn what we need for our little farm. Eventually we are going to buy that land in California to begin our farm. I do want you with me, but I don't want to lose you in the process."

"We are goin' with you, and that's that!" Sara stated with resolve.

And so plans were made by Sam and Sara Horne for their newest life adventure. They would sell anything they had to anyone who had cash. There wasn't much in terms of property, other than the wagon, a couple of horses and a couple of rifles that Sam could afford to leave behind. He would still have his Winchester, but the other rifles were quite a bit older and were a little poorer in quality.

There was also a sum of money that Sara had been saving in one of the banks in Virginia City. After a quick trip to town and the closing of her savings account the family had nearly $150. They could probably get about $200 for the wagon, two draft horses and the two rifles, so that left the Hornes with a tidy sum of close to $350.

From what Sam had heard from other men, they were going to be cutting it very close. He might even have to find work for someone else who needed a strong hand to mine the gold. All Sam knew was that staying in Virginia City, where the silver was playing out and people were leaving for the Yukon Territory, was out of the options for his family. His dream of owning a small farm were resting on his decision to take the risk and head off to the vast frozen land of the north.

All of this weighed heavily on Sam's mind when, at the beginning of April, a small company of people arrived at the barn that the Horne's called home. As they were coming up towards the makeshift house, Sam instantly recognized the one leading the group. It was Pastor Dawkes and four other members of Sam's and Sara's church.

Hugs and greetings were issued, and the pastor stepped up to speak for the others with him, "Well Sam, I see that you three are about to embark on the next chapter of your life's book."

"Yes Pastor, we're almost done here. James Jorie over on F Street came on by this mornin' and bought the wagon and team of horses. Paid me $25 more than what I was hopin' to get for 'em plus sellin' the guns."

"Wonderful, Sam," replied Pastor Dawkes.

"I know for sure that Tom Sikes, over to the feed store, will take the guns off my hands. Probably get nearly $30 for 'em."

"So, Sam, with the sale of the rifles how much are you looking at in terms of cash?" asked Andrew Appleby, another one of the parishioners.

"Best I can figure is that we will have close to $400 to take with us."

"That sounds wonderful, Sam," Pastor Dawkes spoke up. "Before we say all our goodbyes, Sam, we wanted to give you and Sara a little gift. There is just one simple stipulation. We ask that you keep it unopened until you are well on your way to Alaska. There is something mighty important in it that I am sure will come in mighty handily as you are seeking the life the Lord has for you."

"Are you sure you want us to wait that long Pastor?" Sara asked incredulously.

"Absolutely, Sara. That is our one stipulation for you. Please, please, wait until you are well on your journey."

And with that, the pastor of the congregation handed the couple a neatly wrapped box containing God-only-knows-what.

Goodbyes were said, tears were shed, and promises to write were issued as the small party of friends soon left Sam and Sara Horne, and their young boy of almost three years old, Jesse Harlin.

After one last trip through the shed/home they had gratefully been staying in, to make sure that they had not left anything behind, and a cursory look at the houses and structures, the couple boarded the small horse-drawn wagon they had borrowed from the owners of the property where their shed/home stood. They made a quick stop at the feed store to drop off the guns they were selling to Tom Sikes, and then stop and have lunch at the restaurant down the street from the train depot.

Their Reno-bound train was due to depart Virginia City in the evening, and Sam thought it would be best to spend a little time stretching their legs before they would be boarding the train later that night.

Chapter Twelve

At exactly the time scheduled, the grayish-white smoke billowed the locomotive as the Reno-bound train made its way out of Virginia City. Sam and Sara looked out the window of the passenger car they had purchased tickets for, and thoughtfully viewed the desert landscape, not really seeing anything other than memories.

This was going to be an excursion that would take them to Reno, where they would board the San Francisco Challenger, that, as its name implied would take them through small towns such as Verdi, near the California/Nevada border and onto unheard of places such as Boca, Truckee, Soda Springs, Emigrant Gap, Auburn, and many other small settlements until got to Sacramento. Then it would continue through Martinez, Richmond, Berkley, Oakland, and finally arrive at San Francisco about ten hours after leaving Reno.

All there of this small Horne family settled in, on this 13th day of April, for the arduous first leg of an extensive trip into a new and exciting future.

The three men galloped along the tiny road that made its way up the coast of California. They were headed for San Francisco with a completely different purpose than the young family that was making its way across the Sierra Nevada on the night bound passenger train. Whereas the Horne's were setting out to find a bonanza buried beneath the ground, these three men were on their way to San Jose to do a little bit of 'mining' from at least one of the banks in the city. Oh, they were three gifted miners all right. But the mining they did lay in their ability to stake out a bank and hold it up before anyone could alert the law.

It was now April 13th, and Frank Upton, Jake Ashton, and Harry Brindle decide to stop for the evening to eat, finalize the plans for their next heist, and get a good night's sleep. They reined in their horses at a secluded spot just north of Glenwood, on the way to San Jose.

The three set up their camp in short order and, soon have a fire ready to cook whatever it was in the unmarked can food item that they stole from the small store down in Watsonville. Hoping that maybe, just maybe they have stolen something tasteful such as canned meat, they only find that it is nothing more than an unlabeled can of beans.

"Great!" complained Upton. "Another night of canned beans."

"Well, Frank," replied Jake, "at least its edible."

"Barely," came Frank's terse answer.

"Come on, guys," Harry bellowed out. "We pull this next bank job off and it's steak and wine from now on."

"You're right, Harry," said Frank. "With all this gold coming down from Alaska, there must be a ton of it just waitin' for us to grab some."

"Yeah, you got that right, Frank," answered Harry Brindle.

The three of them divided up the unappealing can of beans and set about planning the robbery they were going to do at the First

National Bank of San Jose. Frank had spent some time doing some work around the San Jose area and had a working knowledge of the Bank of San Jose layout. He told the other two that this was going to be a 'sure bet,' and an easy mark. He also assured them that there was no way the law around San Jose was wise enough to catch them. Another day and they would ride out of town, three wealthy men.

The San Francisco Challenger made its way into Auburn, California. The Horne couple could not help but note that they were now in gold country. It was not far from where they were that the gold rush of 1849 took place. Everything in this small town they were now stopping in was built as a reminder to the find at Sutter's Mill. All of what the couple saw was directly related to the find made by James Marshall those short 50 years ago or so.

As they entered the town, they saw the Auburn Iron Works building and the site of the First Transcontinental Railroad. Sam was stirred within by the thought that hundreds of others before him had done just what he and his wife setting out to do. They were settling an undeveloped territory and creating a new place for folks to lay down their roots. But he wasn't too sure how many roots would be laid down in the wilds of Alaska, or how deep those roots could go given that the ground is frozen solid a mere six feet below the surface.

The plan was easy; or at least it was supposed to be so. The bank had the commonly used customer's entrance on the street side, and two back entrances facing an alleyway. Frank was sure that all three doors were kept unlocked during business hours. With that information firmly planted in his mind, he set about explaining what he believed was a fool proof gateway to riches.

"So, the three of us will ride into town and once we get to Santa Clara Street we split up. You two will hitch your horses near the back side of the bank, and station yourselves one at each of the back doors. I will go in through the front main entrance and start a distraction. Once you hear my pistol fire, that is your cue to come on in. We will have everyone surrounded."

"I don't know, Frank." Jake chimed in. "Are you sure that both those back doors will be open?"

"Just listen to me! I've been scouted out this bank now for several weeks. I know that there is a lot of traffic comin' through those back doors. They're gonna' be open."

"Oh, we're believin' you, Jake," Harry added. "We just tryin' to make sure, that's all."

"Listen gents! You can absolutely be sure that I know what I'm sayin' here. We just need to make sure that we keep anyone in that bank from sounding off or calling for help. The constables in San Jose are always patrolling in the banking district, so we have to get in and get out before anyone is the wiser. Okay?"

The other two grumbled their ascent, yet they were not quite sure that this was going to be as easy as Frank Upton was making it out to be. Anything could go wrong.

The train carrying the Horne's began its entry into the portion of land called the Oakland Mole. This was nothing more than an 11,000-foot railroad wharf and ferry pier along the east shore of the San Francisco Bay. Through transfers and maneuvering, the passenger cars of the train were located onto a vessel that would then ferry the entire passenger section of the train across the bay to the western side where San Francisco was located.

Sara was in complete amazement at the whole process. In her entire journey across the country, she had never seen anything quite like this. Sara had never seen anything quite as beautiful as the San Francisco Bay itself. What was amazing to Sara was the large island located about a mile and a half away from the northern shore of San Francisco. She could see the flocks of pelicans that seemed to call this island their home. And she also saw the facility located on the island.

"I believe that there jail-lookin' building is called Camp Alcatraz," stated an older gentleman seated behind the Hornes. "They use it as a long-term detention facility for prisoners of war."

"The whole island looks to me to be a great place to build some kind of prison," Sam joined in the conversation. "Can't see anyone bein' able to escape, no how."

"You might be right, young man," answered the stranger. "The only way to get away from that island is in these waters, and I don't reckon I'd much care to be tryin' to swim the distance it would take to get to dry land."

After their journey aboard the ferry, the cars unloaded on the San Francisco side of the bay, and then they continued the last portion of the journey on to the depot located at Third and Townsend Streets. They took very little time to retrieve their luggage as they had nearly anything to bring from Virginia City. After doing so, the family made their way to a relatively inexpensive hotel in order to wait a few days until it was time to board their steamship which would take them to Fort St. Michael which was located at the delta where the Yukon River fed into the Bering Sea on the western shore of the Nome area of Alaska.

As Murphey's Law has usually been invoked during most major projects, the three would-be bank robbers would soon find out that if anything could go wrong, it would be very bad. Things were going to seriously go wrong, as the trio soon found out.

They rode into San Jose, just as planned, and made their way to the intersection of Santa Clara and Third Streets. Reining their horses to a stop, Frank instructed the other two to make their way down Third Street to the alley way and then proceed down to the backside of the bank which was located on the corner of Santa Clara and First Street.

After watching his two partners head off down to make their way to the back of the bank, Upton urged his horse forward towards his destination. About a block before he reached the front of the bank, he happened upon a young man who was busy working on the engine of one of those new horseless carriages, as they were called. He saw that this one was a model called an Altham. Frank didn't quite understand how these self-propelled gadgets worked, but he knew that they were probably going to make an impact on the new century that would be dawning in a little less than four years. Quietly, he wished the young man good luck as his horse made its way to the bank.

As this was happening, both Jake and Harry had finally made to the back of the bank and tied their horses up to a couple of trees nearby. They both checked their guns to make sure they were ready, and as silently as possible moved towards the two back doors – Jake headed to one and Harry went to the other. They both took a stance near their respective door and waited for Frank's gun to be fired, signaling them to make their entrance.

The next few minutes were a blur for Frank. In a moment everything was headed in a direction that he could neither change nor control. Exactly as Upton had entered the bank, the young man who was tinkering with his Altham auto started it up and quickly jumped behind the steering lever to start off down the street in front of the bank. Just as Frank was beginning to fire the distraction shot into the air, a loud backfire from the car sounded outside on the street. Both Jake and Harry, who were ready, guns in hand, to barge into the bank and assist Frank in the hold up. But of all things, both doors were locked, and the two men were unable to burst through to aide their partner.

In the time being, thinking that the police had fired a shot, Frank quickly retreated through the front door of the building, gun in hand and ready to shoot. Without taking time to assess the situation, Upton immediately panicked and began firing his gun wildly, just as some police officers were coming to investigate.

Seeing a man wildly firing a pistol towards people who were innocently walking down the street caused them to return fire upon Upton, both officers true to their training, were able to hit the bank robber squarely in the chest. Frank went down in a heap – dead!

With all the firing of guns they heard around in front of the bank, both Harry Brindle and Jake Ashton, would be professional bank robbers, looked at each other and without a word ran to their horses to get out as quickly as they could. Things had definitely 'gone south' very quickly. They had to get out and get out fast!

So, the two men rode as fast as they could to cover the little more than forty-one miles to San Francisco. Right now, they needed to be somewhere there were a lot of people. San Francisco was the perfect place to get lost in a crowd around this part of California.

Sam came back to the hotel room after arranging passage aboard a vessel that would take them to the Yukon. He seemed to be a little forlorn as he sat down at the small table next to the bed that Sara had been lying on with young Jesse. Their son had seemed to be a little under the weather all morning, so Sara had chosen to stay with him in the room as Sam made the travel arrangements.

Sara asked him, "Sam, is anything wrong? Were you able to get passage?"

"In a way," he replied, with a sigh.

"You sound as if something is awful wrong, Sam. I've been through a lot, my dear husband, if you didn't realize, and I can take pretty near anything bad you could tell me. Whatever is wrong is nothin' we can't make it through. So, what's the matter, Sam?"

"Well, it seems that we both miscalculated the cost of our trip, Sara. It seems that a lot of folks are making their fortunes off of those of us who are just trying to make a life for ourselves."

"What's that mean, Sam?"

"Well Sara, dear, it seems that it's costing us nearly all we had saved up just to have the opportunity to work our way on board a ship for Alaska."

"Work our way? Why?"

"You know that steamship called the Excelsior – the one we that would only cost us about $40 for a small cabin?"

"I remember, Sam."

"It's so booked up now that we wouldn't be able to get to St. Michael until November at the earliest. That's way too late to get started in the freezing weather up there, and anyway, we would pretty much run out of money down here just waiting."

"So, what do we do, Sam?" Sara asked, realizing the seriousness of their situation. "Do we just go back to Virginia City, like beaten dogs?"

"Well, no, not exactly."

"Just tell me Sam. What are we going to do?"

"Darling," responded the big man who was beginning to feel smaller and smaller, "I was able to get us aboard another ship going north, but we won't have but a few dollars left when we get to St. Michael."

"But we would still be able to get to Alaska, won't we, Sam? That sounds like a good thing to me."

"Sara, I had to pay nearly $300 so that the two of us can work our way on board the ship," Sam revealed with a saddened and defeated tone.

"What kind of work, Sam?"

"Seems like they always need help in the kitchen, you know, cookin' and all. And I'll be working in the engine room keepin' the boilers fired up. I'll be able to watch Jesse during the day while you're working and then I will help down in the engine room at night."

"Sounds to me like we just paid for the privilege of workin' on the ship. Well, we will do what we must do, Sam. At least we are still on our way and that is all that matters."

And so, they both embraced each other and felt the comfort and closeness of one another. They were more determined than ever to follow their dreams as a young, strong family.

The two trail-ridden desperadoes were seated at a table, devouring their meals as if they had not had one in a week. Jake and

Harry had indeed ridden hard to get to San Francisco from their failed bank heist down in San Jose. It was obvious to them that the attempted bank robbery was indeed far outside their expertise. The entire episode was a fiasco, and it was beyond time that they both get back to what they did profoundly well. They needed to find what they called a mark, or more commonly referred to as a victim, and perform a confidence job upon them.

Almost anything anyone could talk about wherever the two conmen went was the discovery of large amounts of gold in Alaska and the Yukon Territory. But finding gold in Alaska did not have any appeal to Harry and Jake. It required so much less effort to find an easy mark and pluck the money right out of their bank accounts. Many people were so ignorant they were being cheated that they would go out of their way to accommodate their predators.

So, the two men discussed and agreed upon the best way that they would get the money they needed to set sail for the distant north. They would find a gullible soul, help themselves to the dollars they needed to book passage on one of the many northbound ships, and once there, they would start to really glean the low-hanging fruit. It is true that they had a minor setback in San Jose, but now they were on track to make a sterling comeback.

The Horne family made their way to the empty table near the center of a small dinner near their hotel. While Sam and Sara, who was carrying Jesse, passed through the dining room, they noticed at the table adjacent to theirs the two rough looking men talking to each other and gulping down their food. Sara thought it was odd how hungry both men seemed to be. She would not be surprised to see them eating the very plates, by watching how they were attacking their dinner.

"I hope that both those men get their fill. It's too bad there isn't some kind of "all-you-can-eat" restaurant somewhere," Sara commented as they sat at their own table.

"I'm not sure a restaurant can be much of a success if it were to allow people to keep eating and eating and eating," Sam added.

"It'd be an interesting idea though, if it could be worked out."

The young married couple then set to ordering and eating the delivered dinner. During the meal, they discussed how they would make the best of their new travel plans. Yes, they would have to work to pay their travel expenses, and yes, they were now going to be left with very little money to afford the necessary items they would need, but it also seemed that every time a door closed on their plans, new openings were provided.

Chapter Thirteen

It hadn't taken very long before Jake Ashton and Harry Brindle gleaned a wealth of information from the young couple seated at the table next to them. Overhearing bits and pieces of the conversation between the man and woman allowed them to learn that they were indeed on their way to the gold fields in Alaskan Territory, and that they had booked passage on a steamship called the Arctic Queen.

It was more than apparent that these two were not at all wealthy, and right now they could offer nothing worth their time and efforts. But that was right now, and the way they were going to work would be a process of gaining the couple's friendship, setting up an enterprise together with them, and then, when they least expected it, they would strike. If they ever felt remorse for the 'cons' that they pulled on unsuspecting targets, well it was a dog-eat-dog world and anyway, these two were young, they would learn their lesson, and more than likely, they would be able to recoup their losses.

More than likely, the Arctic Queen was filled with passengers, so Jake and Harry were determined to book passage on a vessel that was leaving soon after the Queen. At any rate, the targets were chosen, and the course had been set. Now it was just a matter of gaining the trust of the two unsuspecting targets.

Finally! It was, by now mid-July. Sam, Sara, and Jesse were now fully recruited and serving aboard the Arctic Queen, which was on its way to Fort St. Michael, Alaska. Both Sam and his young wife had gotten used to their new roles aboard the vessel. They were both literally working day and night, Sam in the boiler room and Sara in the galley. The work was arduous for both of them, but they had little time to rue their current situation. Yes, it was true that they were working harder than they ever had in the past, but at least they were getting closer to where they intended to be – the gold fields in the Yukon.

Both Sam and Sara agreed that life would be a little easier if things were a little more normal. It was extremely difficult getting used to the ever-lengthening daylight conditions. Now, in early-July and at this extreme northern latitude, the sun would not begin setting until nearly 1:00 a.m., and then begin to rise a mere four hours later at 5:00 in the morning. They were very thankful for the heavy blackout curtains over the portholes. At least they could get a few hours' sleep.

Jesse was now a toddling 3-year-old boy. What made it especially difficult for his mother and father was that he was also extremely curious. Being on board this floating wonder world was a nothing less than a sensory wonder world for the young lad. It was a task to keep him from interrupting the first-class passengers, but by the time the ship had been underway a few days, everyone had gotten used to the little man. Some of those on board found Jesse's antics enough to break the monotony of the hours sailing a seemingly boundless sea.

Within a couple of weeks, the ship began maneuvering through the Aleutian Island chain. Off to the right, or starboard side, as the

Horne's soon learned, was the small location named Pavlof Harbor. Further away on the other side of the ship was Unalaska Island. There was nothing incredible about either of these two land masses, except that the older, more experienced crew members warned Sam that there was likely to be some rough sailing for the next few days. They tried to explain the currents and the alternating winds to the young man, but all he knew was that things might get somewhat harsh for a few days. They had better secure as much down in their small cabin as they possibly could. They didn't have much, but they still valued the things that they brought with them. As he thought about this, it suddenly dawned on him that they had still not opened the package that Pastor Dawkes had given to them. Surely, they were far enough away from Virginia City to go ahead and reveal what was lovingly given to them in what seem to be a very long time ago.

Sam did not have time or the opportunity to remind Sara about the package. True to the warnings from his coworkers, the seas were becoming unsettled. The changes occurred at a fast pace, and it was 'all-hands-on-deck' for every seaman, on or off duty. While the crew members were busy doing all they could to keep the craft moving through the rough seas, the passengers were all confined to their cabins. Since nothing could be done for the meal prepping, the galley crew, including Sara, was informed that they should also go to and remain in their cabins.

As they were trying to stumble their way towards the crew cabins, Sara encountered a fellow galley worker who said in an optimistic way, "don't worry, dear. After a few months of this you will get used to this passage. Thank God it doesn't last forever!"

"Oh, my husband and I won't have to get used to this. We're getting off at Fort St. Michael. We're headed for the gold fields."

"You sure 'bout that, dear?"

"What do you mean," Sara asked, a little bit hesitantly.

"Well, I was on my way to the gold fields with my husband more than six months ago. Just like you and Sam, we booked passage on this ship, and had to work our way up to Alaska because we didn't quite have the amount we needed to board as regular passengers. Seems that they also require something they didn't tell us about when we started out. Everyone who sails on this ship as working passengers are required to pay a $250 debarkation fee upon arrival."

Fear spread upon the face of Sara, as she listened to her coworker explain the nightmare that trapped many unsuspecting souls.

"Does your husband work down in the boiler room with my Sam?" Sara inquired.

"My husband jumped overboard when we found out. He told me he would rather die than be a slave aboard this here floating prison ship. I am sure that if he didn't drown, he most certainly froze to death in these waters. My only regret is that I didn't jump over with him."

Sara finally retrieved Jesse from the first-aid office, where the kind doctor was watching him, and holding onto his hand to steady him, she made it back to her quarters. Tears were flowing down her face as she thought about what she was told. She was sure that Sam was not informed about this 'debarkation' fee, as she was told. She was also sure, without a doubt, that they did not have the money they needed to debark from the ship. It might have cost her new friend and her husband $250, but she could be very sure that dollar amount had only gone up in the last six months.

It was satisfying to know that the shell game still worked. It worked especially well when your mark has had a few drinks under his belt. It also helped matters out for Jake and Harry that they had worked for a couple of years with the traveling carnival show. A lot of people attributed P. T. Barnum with saying that there was a sucker born every minute, but there were a couple of other men who might have been the first to say it. Whether it was Barnum or more likely Joseph Bessemer, it was still true. There were plenty of gullible people out there just begging to be fleeced.

The two men ran the con as smoothly as anyone could and before long, they had more than enough cash to book passage on a ship that left San Francisco a week after the Arctic Queen.

As their ship neared the calm waters of the Aleutian Island chain, they could hear people talking about how rough the waters here had been just one week ago. They said that another vessel had nearly been capsized as it sailed passed Unalaska Island. No one was sure what had happened to the ship, but both Jake and Harry were determined to find out as soon as they could. Surely someone on board this ship would be able to find out the name of the ship and what had happened to it.

It had been one of the worst times that Sam and Sara had experienced since beginning their quest. Sam had confirmed that they would indeed have to present the captain of the ship another $350 that they did not possess to be able to debark from the ship. That was almost a moot point when the ship had nearly been ravaged by a storm and nearly everyone came very close to being lost at sea. Even when it was not apparent to the Horne's, they were still under the watchful eye of a loving and providential Heavenly Father.

That God was keeping the family firmly guarded in his loving hands was the farthest thought from Sam or Sara, as they open their luggage and boxes containing all their belongings and set everything out so they could take stock of what they had. What they saw laid out before them was a sad story of their life up to this point. At least many of the others on board the ship would think so. Besides a couple of changes of clothes and some warm, fur-lined coats that were a necessity in the Yukon, there was scant else. The list of items was not long at all: Sara's bible, a thimble that had belonged to her grandmother. Jesse had two or three small toys that he would play with, and Sam's contribution to their earthly possessions were a few souvenir coins from the Columbian Exposition of 1893, and he also had a medal that his father received from service in the Civil War. This seemed to be a sad, sad legacy.

Then, Sam remembered the gift box that their pastor from Virginia City had given them. There was no better time than now to open it to see what their church family had given them. Tearing the tape that held the box flaps firmly in place, allowed Sam to access the contents within. Neatly stacked within the box were photographs of some of the church members, a few notes wishing them all well, some toys that Jesse could play with, and at the bottom of the box Sam found an official looking envelop that looked like it might contain something more than a letter. On this envelop the words "To the Horne Family" and it looked like something just short of being a legal document.

Sam held the envelop up so Sara could see the address, and said, "Well Sara, this looks a might official!"

"Don't just hold it there, Sam. Open it up and see what's in it."

So, Sam did exactly as his wife said, and slowly and carefully tore open the letter.

Upon opening it, a bound stack of money slipped out onto the bed and Sam was holding an enclosed letter in his hand. He opened the letter and began to read what it said.

To Sam Horne and family,

Mr. Horne, you do not know me very well, so let me introduce myself. I am Andrew Sanders, the father of Phillip Sanders, with whom I know that you are very familiar.

First, please let me apologize for the grief that my son put both you and your wife through. I tried to do my best to raise Phillip to respect others and to do whatever he could to be gracious and loving towards. I do not what went wrong with Phillip, but I do know that he did his best to terrorize people that he thought were beneath him. The way he treated others grieved both his mother and me.

Mr. Horne, I do know that what was reported that happened on the night of his death was probably inaccurate. More than likely, rather than trying to help you put out the fire, my son was the one who caused the fire. I appreciate how you may have been a little liberal towards Philip, but there is one thing that I know, and that is how childish and mean my son could be.

Second, I know that Philip has caused you and your family excessive financial grief. I am enclosing cash within this letter to help you recover what you may have lost through my son's actions. You should find a sum of $4,000 in one-hundred-dollar notes. Please accept this as a gift for your kindness and concern for my family's reputation.

Sincerely,
Andrew Sanders.

Sam slowly picked up the bound banknotes, removed the binding, and counted the bills. True to his word, there was $4,000 in the stack.

With glistening eyes and a quivering voice, Sam said to Sara, "I don't think we will be staying on as the captain's servants, Sara. There is more than enough to pay our 'debarkation bill', and we have a substantial amount for what we need in our new life in the gold fields."

"I think that our Lord is still watching over us, Sam."

"I know that he is, Sara."

Jake and Harry knew that the captain of the ship would have information regarding the Arctic Queen. So, on a fair, bright morning a couple of days after they set sail, Harry happened to run into the captain on the fore deck of the steamer.

"Sir," Harry began. "My friend and I have a mutual acquaintance onboard the vessel that left a few days before us. I believe the name of the ship is the Arctic Queen. Do you have any information as to how that ship is doing? I believe they might have gotten caught up in that storm that we heard about farther up north."

"Well, it didn't look very good for the Queen. They nearly went down, but the captain is a friend of mine, and a very fine seaman. He was able to navigate through the Aleutian Island chain, and now I think they are just a few hours ahead of us and nearing Fort St. Michael."

"That is such good news, Captain. Thank you."

"You bet, sir. If you keep a good watch, you just might catch sight of your friend soon. The storm put them off course a little and allowed up to catch up with them. Just keep watching the port side," he said, indicating the left side of the ship.

But the Arctic Queen was held up a little bit further behind than was assumed by the captain of the other ship. So, even though they left a few days after the Horne family, Jake and Harry were docking in the port at Fort St. Michael a full two hours before the Arctic Queen.

Not wanting to lose their marks, Harry and Jake decided to remain on board their vessel until the Queen had moored and was unloading passengers. There was really no hurry for them to get off the ship, at least until the Horne's had made it in safely. So, they both waited patiently for the arrival of the other vessel.

They did not have long to wait. The Arctic Queen could soon be seen from the vantage point of the citadel of Ft. St. Michael, which was located just above Saint Michael Bay. Not wanting to miss their marks, the two rogues quickly made their way to the dock where they had recently debarked from the vessel that had brought them there.

With all their possessions packed up and ready to be removed from Arctic Queen, Sam took $400 from the letter from Mr. Sanders, and stored away the remaining $3,600 in a satchel he had retrieved from the engine room. Then he carefully stowed this packet in the lining of their locking trunk and made sure that it was indeed locked. He would take no chances with this captain of the Arctic Queen. The best plan was to have plenty of witnesses to the transaction he was about to complete.

Sam and Sara found the captain on the deck, and as he hoped, at least ten passengers and a few crew members were around talking with the captain. Without any hesitation, Sam approached the pilot of the ship to confront him.

"So, Captain, let me completely understand what you recently told me," Sam began his discourse.

"Yes, yes Horne, what is it that you need?" the captain responded.

"Well sir, as I recall you said that there was a $350 debarkation fee for my family to be able to move on off this ship; is that correct, sir?"

"As a matter of fact, the price to remove yourself from the Queen is now $400, Horne."

Knowing that there were all the witnesses he needed to hold the captain to his extortionary plan, Sam withdrew the four $100 bills from his pocket, and handing them over to the captain he said, "Sir, would you be so kind as to count out the money I just gave you to confirm that it is the required total."

Seeing that there was the agreed on quoted amount, and knowing that there were more than enough people, including honest citizens watching the whole course of affairs, the captain had no other alternative than to hand over the needed paperwork for the Horne family, along with all their possessions, to leave the ship when it was secured to the dock.

So, Sam, Sara, and their little toddler Jesse were released from the clutches of the master of the Arctic Queen. They quickly secured all their earthly possessions to a small cart which was to be used for passenger belongings and made their way to the gangway for disembarkation. As they neared the passageway, Sara saw the captain who was trying to avoid any eye contact with either her or Sam.

"By the way, captain," Sara spoke up, "we are heading to the office of the fort in charge of the ship operations here. There is a young woman working aboard this vessel who you've been keeping a prisoner for almost half a year. And I am sure she is not the only one. I'm pretty sure that there are some strong charges that can be brought against someone like a ship's captain who deliberately steals people's lives away."

At hearing that, the captain took on a frightened expression, and he quickly slipped away towards the pilot house. Hopefully, Sara thought, several others will be leaving this floating prison.

Jake and Harry kept watch of each of the passengers who were walking down the gangway towards the dock and then to the processing center. It was very important for them to keep a close eye out on the passengers so that they could recognize the couple. It should be fairly easy for them to be spotted because of the size of the man and because, as they had overheard the couple talking at the table in San Francisco, there would also be a small boy in tow. Once they spotted the three, they Jake and Harry would silently slip in behind them and follow them to the next stage of their journey. The important thing for them to do was to make sure they did not become separated from the three.

Within a few minutes, their marks were acquired, making their way in line slowly down the ramp. Moving was quickly as they could while remaining inconspicuous, Jake Ashton and Harry Brindle quickly removed themselves from where they were staked out and moved to the area behind the processing center where they knew from their own experience that the Horne's would end up before being moved to the barracks they had already been in for the last half day. There was still plenty of empty billets in the structure, certainly more than enough to house this incoming group. Tomorrow would be the next time the steamboat with the sidewinder paddles began its journey around St. Michael Island, across the North Pacific within a couple of miles of shore, and then finally entering the Yukon River at the outlet just below Pienluk Island. This was going to be the final thousand miles or so of their quest to the gold fields near Fort Yukon in the center of the massive Alaskan Territory.

Soon the two scoundrels had relocated themselves to a large quad area behind the processing center building. It should have been much harder for them to not get into the area that the newly arrived people would be directed to, but most of the soldiers from the fort tasked with watching out for would-be intruders were very inattentive and distracted by their idle talk among themselves. At any rate, Jake and Harry would remain discretely hidden until arriving passengers and soon-to-be stampeders.

The line moved at a snail's pace as one at a time the passengers were processed into the territory. There were nearly forty people including the Horne family, and so they each had to be verified by any official document that showed residence in the United States. Without exception, everyone was able to present the proper documentation which could be any mail showing that they had lived in one of the forty-five states or three territories to the south. Thankfully, there were no problems for Sam, Sara and their son Jesse to be admitted on to the waiting area in the rear of the building.

Of course, once a majority of folk had congregated in the holding quad, Harry and Jake emerged from the secluded area and began making their way to contact the Horne's. Finally, the hook was set as the two scoundrels had set the hook and began conversation with both Sara and Sam.

"I seem to remember you from the place where we were eating back in, ... where was it, Sam?" Sara asked her husband.

"Well Sara, I reckon that you and me has eaten in quite a few places in the last few weeks."

"Wait, now I remember. Don't you recall, Sam? You know how we saw these two here with such a big appetite, remember?"

"Oh yeah! That was back down in San Francisco, ... I think," Sam recalled.

"Say!" Jake exclaimed, "I remember that. You know Harry. It was that night that we got there from San Jose."

"Sure, sure. I do recall bein' a bit famished. If I'm not mistaken, we had just gotten out o' San Jose in a rush and were nearly starvin'. Seemed like a month since we had eaten anything other than beans."

"That's right! It's all comin' back now," Jake responded. "We were kind a' in a hurry to get on board a ship bound for Alaska."

Nodding, Harry asked the young couple, "So you two were lookin' to come up here too, I see."

"That's right," said Sam. "Along with everyone else here we're takin' the Bella tomorrow morning, and hopefully we will be gettin' to Fort Yukon in about a week. It's kinda' late in the year, but I'm thinkin' that maybe we can get settled in someplace near the fort, and there might be a little work around there. I do know that we're going to have to get stocked up on supplies and a way to pack 'em into the fields."

Harry and Jake stood there listening to him talk and taking in the plans that the Horne family had created for themselves. As they listened to Sam, they would eye each other knowing that this would be an easy set up. Sure, it might require a little bit of work on their part, but if they played their cards right a fortune could be made at Sam and Sara Horne's expense. The secret to their success would be in gaining the confidence of this young couple. That would also be easy.

The bait was on the line and the fish were on the hook. It was just a matter of pulling in the victims and landing their catch.

Chapter Fourteen

So, the destination was Fort Yukon, located about 140 miles north of the new town of Fairbanks, situated on the Yukon River. Because they were moving against the current, the maximum speed they could attain was around 8 miles per hour. So, with agile navigating around sand bars and dead-end channels, it was going to take about 2 weeks to traverse the nine hundred or so miles from Fort St. Michael to Fort Yukon.

There were many things that Jake and Harry could do in the meantime to gain the trust of their new acquaintances. Right away Jake knew that Sara had a strong Christian faith. It was also clearly apparent that Sam was not too far behind when it came to trusting their God. There was hardly a day that went by, but which Sara would not brooch the subject of her Christian faith and the teachings written in the Bible. Jake could clearly see how profoundly and deeply rooted in Scriptures the two lived their lives. Just seeing the big, six-foot plus frame of a man sporting a bible and from time to time referring to it in his every day conversations seem unbelievable. Both Sara and Sam were more like missionaries on board the vessel rather than stampeders who were seeking their fortune.

"Well," Harry thought to himself, "as far as I'm concerned, all that does is make the Horne family a much easier mark. Nothing more easily hoodwinked than a bible-thumping person of faith."

Harry pondered that this was going to be so easy. With the help of his idiot partner, Jake, he would play the game against these greenhorns, take them down when they least expected it, double-cross his partner Jake, and finally disappear with all the cash he would extract from the gold in these rubes.

It was now the first week of September 1897, as everyday life aboard the Bella became more and more routine. The one big change that did not take much getting used to was the length of the sunlight during the days. Yes, indeed the sun did not set until nearly 10 o'clock at night, but at least it did not rise until 7:30 the next morning – a full nine and a half hours of night darkness. Yes, is it made for a long day of nearly fourteen hours of sunlight, but at least there was plenty of darkness to get a good night's sleep. And since neither Sam nor Sara were working aboard the vessel as they had been on the Arctic Queen, they both were in much better shape, physically and mentally.

This was not to say that from time to time the passengers did not have to contribute in some way. Whenever an uncharted and unexpected sand bar caught the vessel, everyone except the small children were needed to help free the boat from the entrapment. At least all of this had been explained to the passengers prior to sailing, so no one was caught off guard, and everyone pitched in as well as they could. For Sam, it was nothing more than a chance to strengthen his body for the arduous task ahead of mining his future out of the Alaskan ground.

Neither Harry nor Jake were anywhere as compliant with helping. They both grumbled anytime the least amount of work presented itself. Complaining became second nature to both men.

Their groanings became so common that most people on board the boat found every way possible to stay away from them. Sadly, this also meant that Sara was avoided by the others because it always seemed that wherever she was one could count on Harry or Jake being there.

But it was all part of the game to the swindlers. Stick close to their mark, build up a rapport with them, and then snare them into the trap. They would stick to the Horne family like honey sticks to toast.

Before the daily routine aboard the Bella was reduced to sheer monotony, everyone on board could see that the boat was nearing the destination – Fort Yukon. Not nearly standing as stately as the citadel of Fort St. Michael, nevertheless, it was a tremendous relief for all on board the vessel.

Surprisingly, nestled next to nearly every barrack was some sort of water vessel – a small rowboat, or some other item that could serve to keep oneself high and dry. Sara and Sam were extremely pleased when they spotted several retail businesses that were there to service the soldiers, stampeders, and the local itinerate people. These people were mostly of the Athabascan tribe and made up a large proportion of the area's population. The soldiers stationed at Fort Yukon served as much to protect the villages of these native clans as it did to protect the miners from each other. Sadly, as much problem the stampeders had with each other was only magnified by the problems caused by such a sudden influx of gold seekers. To the miners, the area meant only one thing – a way to strike it rich. To the native Athabascan the region meant home; a home that had to be defended.

Nevertheless, since it would not be until the thaw of spring next year until the Horne's could move out into the fields to mine, it would be nice if either Sara or Sam could find a little bit of work to do. At least Sam had an adequate amount of knowledge about working with draft animals and farming, and Sara had an entire lifetime of experience working in a retail store. Surely, between the two of them, they could find enough work to enable them to build up their supplies for next spring as they set out to make a mining claim.

Unfortunately, as they settled into their daily routine at Fort Yukon, getting a billet and preparing for the deep winter, there was always an awareness of Jake Ashton and Harry Brindle. They never seemed more than an earshot away from them. It was not that they moved into their small bungalow to live with them, but it just seemed like they were always there.

From time to time, the topic of the presence of these two men came up between Sam and Sara. It was apparent to both of them that these two previous strangers in their lives were now becoming a fixed feature of most of their waking hours.

One day Sam was ruminating about their daily presence, and he spoke out, "I tell ya, Sara. I'm getting' a might bit tired of always having Jake and Harry underfoot. Maybe I need to have a little talk with 'em 'bout it."

"I know, Sam, I know! But I'm not so sure that it's a good idea to go chasin' 'em off so quickly. We're lookin' at some mighty hard work out there in the fields next spring and summer. Might be good to team up with both of them, don't ya' think?"

"You mean settin' up a claim together?"

"Well Sam, we can't carry all the gold out o' here. There is plenty to go around, don't ya' think. Besides, many hands make the liftin' lighter."

"I'll think on that, Sara. You are probably right, though."

And so, they settled in for the long, cold winter ahead. One thing that would not stop, regardless of how cold it got, was the need for food and consumable supplies such as heating fluid and repairs of broken tools. Some of the stampeders that had arrived in the past year were those whose dream was not to mine for gold, but to make their fortune selling needed supplies to the miners.

Jonah and Betty Skyler were just one example of these many entrepreneurs. They were an older couple who had arrived in the previous spring of 1897, bringing with them a large supply of items that would be sold in the coming winter. These supplies were non-perishables, including canned foods and preserves. They had been able to secure a large structure for the purposes of establishing a merchandise store. Through the summer and autumn, they were able to begin selling their merchandise, and while the boats could get to Fort Yukon, they were able to resupply.

It did not take long for Sara to gain employment with the Skyler's because of her lifetime of experience working in mercantile stores – both at her parents in Bensenville, and during the time she was living in Virginia City. They also saw that Sam would be an asset to their store by providing handyman work around the place and repairing maintaining miners' equipment. Spades always needed to be sharpened. Sleds needed to be fixed. Even wagons were used during the summer and fall months and often became broken, needing repair.

What was especially endearing to Sara was the way in which the Skyler's had taken to her son Jesse. They had become the grandparents that he so desperately needed in his young life. Soon, everywhere that Jonah Skyler went, one could see Jesse following along with him. It was such a touching sight, yet at the same time Sara knew that come spring they would be heading out to stake a claim for themselves. She hoped that it would not be too traumatic for either the Skyler's or her son.

As usual, Jake and Harry were busy. But they were not busy at being productive – far from it. They were finding as many ways to rob and steal as there were people living at Fort Yukon. To the two men it was just a matter of biding their time. Spring was on its way, and the fruit would be exceedingly ripe.

Chapter Fifteen

There are times when certain events happen that will forever alter the course of your life. Oddly, most of those times go unrecognized as life-altering events. They are usually seen as just another thing in a long string of events that make up what we call our day. Still, this is what happened to Sara and Sam one cold, dark November evening in 1897.

While walking back to her billet from a long hard day at the Skyler's supply store, she heard a slight commotion taking place, and soon saw a tattered and worn looking elderly, ebony-skinned man emerging from around the corner just before the street to her bungalow. Closely behind the man there was a gang of Caucasian men who were doing all they could to harass the older gentleman, who only seemed to be trying to get away from these younger, more disruptive vagrants.

Suddenly, an emptied bottle of some type of beverage – most likely alcoholic in nature – was thrown at the old man, glancing off the side of his head. He staggered slightly, and Sara could see a formation of blood beginning to ooze down his neck. Yet, the old man still tried to continue moving away from the young men, but they kept up with him tying to cause him problems, if they in anyway could.

Then the racist epithets began. Vicious, spiteful names were thrown at the man who was the same as the rest of the gathered crowd – a image bearer of Almighty God. But the vile words emanating from the heart of these young and ignorant fools showed to everyone that they did not have much of a high opinion of God's creation.

Sara had seen enough. As the commotion continued down the street toward a warehouse, she sprinted toward her lodging. She knew that Sam would be able to help the older Negro man. More than likely, all that was needed was the appearance of a large, threatening-looking man would show up to defend the old gentleman.

Breaking through the doorway of their bungalow Sara yelled out to her husband, "Sam! Sam! You've got to help him. They're going to kill the man!"

"Sara, what is the problem?"

"Oh Sam, it was just awful. I just saw a poor, old, colored man being attacked by a gang of thugs. Sam, the old man is tryin' his best to get free o' them, but they just keep followin' and botherin' him."

"Where did you say he is, Sara?"

"Last I saw, he was turnin' down to go to the old warehouse. Sam they're gonna' kill the poor old man if someone don't stop 'em."

At those instructions, Sam quickly jumped up, put his fur-lined coat on, grabbed a large club-like stick standing next to the door, and headed out of the room towards the old warehouse.

Trying to run as fast as he could without falling on the ice and breaking an arm or leg, Sam finally got to the location that Sara told him the crowd was herding the innocent old man. Upon arriving, the sight that Sam beheld was frightening. Things had escalated, and the young men had tied a noose around the neck of the older man. It was very apparent that there was soon going to be a lynching, and all Sam knew was that he had to stop it. The man was going to lose his life for nothing more than the color of his skin.

Without any hesitation, and with no one else there to help him, Sam threw himself into the fray. The club became a formidable weapon. Swinging wildly at any and every person within reach, he soon had the better hand of the situation. The younger men soon realized that this new participant in the little game they were playing was a force to be reckoned with. In a matter of just a few minutes, three young gang members lay unconscious on the ground, and all the rest fled from the place, most nursing some wound administered by Sam Horne.

When the 'dust settled,' Sam was doing all that he could to administer aid to the old man. He helped to steady him on his feet, found a scrap of clean cloth to apply to the wound on his head, and to get him to the bungalow that Sara and he were living in, and then to figure out what to do next. He was sure that Sara would be able to treat any wound that might be serious. Since there were no doctors or other medical professionals around, being able to perform minor surgery such as sewing up wounds was an essential talent to have.

It turned out that the older man who was attacked by the young gang was a sixty-year-old, former slave from Louisiana named Amos Sutter. He did not quite know his exact age, but he did know that his former master had told him that Andrew Jackson had already started his second term as President of the United States when

Amos was born. That was in 1834, so by rudimentary calculations, he was probably around sixty-three years old.

As Sara tended to the wounds Amos had received, she couldn't help but notice his gentle and kind spirit. Sam would often remark about how infuriating those young men and their ilk were, and every time he did, Amos replied that it was most likely because of their age or lack of understanding that they treated other people like that.

"Yeah, but you see, Mr. Sutter, ..." Sam responded.

"Please, just call me Amos," came his reply.

"Okay, but Amos I've had dealings with these types of fellows for a while now. Sure, they are young, but that is no excuse to treat other people like animals. They understand completely what they are doing. They understand it now just as their fathers did back in the sixties."

"Well sir, you may be rightly true in what you say," answered Amos.

"Are you wantin' to do mining out in the fields, Amos?" Sara interjected.

"I's wantin' to do anything that they is to be done. I jist lookin' for work somewhere."

"Amos, I think that I might be able to get some work for you. I am pretty sure that it would not be nearly as strenuous as tryin' to make a go of it out in the mines."

"That be right kind of you, missy."

"Listen, Amos. If we are to call you Amos, the least thing you could do for us is to call us by our given names also. You call me Sara, that's Sam my husband there, and the young'un's name is Jesse."

"I thank ye, Miss Sara."

True to her words, Sara was able to get work for Amos at the Skyler's store. She convinced Jonah and Betty that as soon as spring arrived, her and Sam would be heading out to the gold fields with his two partners, trying to make a decent strike. Things were probably going to get a lot busier in the new year and Amos would be a tremendous asset.

The storekeepers agreed and started training Amos in all the duties that he would have to do. Amos was working, the Skyler's were becoming more and more prosperous, and the Horne's were getting anxious for the early thaws and the opportunity for Sam, Jake, and Harry to try to find a vein of gold.

Chapter Sixteen

Thankfully, the long, cold winter was beginning to slow, and signs of the warmer portion of the year were approaching. It was no surprise to anyone in this region of the world that the weather would suddenly turn warm, and people could shed their coats. The average temperature in the warmest month of July was a mere 59° F, but compared to the months of winter, that was downright balmy.

At any rate, during the passage of December through to March, the Horne's, Ashton, and Brindle had informally become a partnership of sorts. After several meetings and much discussion, they agreed that Sara and Jesse would remain behind in Fort Yukon while the other three – Sam, Jake, and Harry – would set off as early as possible to try to find a possible bonanza. The boy needed to stay somewhere relatively safe, and he needed his mother to remain with him. Sara reluctantly agreed even though, to her, it seemed that she was having to sacrifice the most in this new partnership. After all, it was she who would have to wait, not knowing the fate of her husband, and having to protect Jesse and herself from the unknown factors that were 'out there.'

But the threats to her or the boy were miniscule, compared to the dangers that they would have been exposed to in the search for gold. So, she finally relented to this plan. Jonah and Betty Skyler would offer safety, and she would be able to keep a watchful eye on her son.

Sara was also concerned about how Amos was going to be able to survive the next few months at Fort Yukon. The incident at the warehouse last November was more than a wakeup call for her. There were hateful people everywhere. She spent what felt like a lifetime looking after the wellbeing of the downtrodden, and this was no exception. She, along with many others in her small church, had done their best to make Soninka and Janos Polchev, the real parents of Jesse, feel accepted and protected. She had even given up her life and family in Bensenville to give Jesse a chance at a normal life.

Sara remembered what Sam was like before the Lord began using her to lead him to a relationship with Jesus. She was privileged to watch this confused and, at times, volatile man become a gentle giant who gave his life over to the service of Christ.

So, in a way, Sara knew that she would be best used by the Lord by staying right where she was and making sure that Amos was kept safe.

As April had finally proved to be a true beginning to the warm months and not a false start—as was so often the case—everyone in the settlement knew that it was time for partings. Many women besides Sara Horne would be staying at the fort, and so the tears were flowing as, one by one the men began to filter out of the settlement, taking their pack animals, and beginning the quest for the elusive metal that had brought them all the way to the northern reaches of the world.

Holding on to her husband with Jesse gently squeezed in between them, Sara whispered in his ear, "I will sorely miss you, Sam. I love you, ya. know?"

"Yes, I do know that more than I know anything. Take good care of yourself and the boy, Sara."

And with one last kiss before letting her go, Sam knelt beside Jesse and gave him a big bear hug. "You take care of your mama, son."

And then he turned and led the pack mule away to join up with his partners, who had dismissed themselves from the two for the purpose of the farewell.

So now a new episode was beginning for Sara Horne, as she watched her husband and his partners fade into three small dots on the horizon, and finally there was nothing that she could see.

Wiping the tears from her eyes, Sara turned and scooped up Jesse who needed to be consoled because he too knew that his daddy would be gone for some time. Sara held him tightly and walked slowly back to the bungalow that had been their home for the last few months. She prayed that it would be a short wait and she would soon get a message from one of the partners that they had struck gold.

Life in the fort had changed dramatically as the last of the miners set in their search for riches. There were still plenty of souls left to inhabit the little village, but it seemed that the mood of the people had changed. Thankfully, the drunken reveries had all but vanished, as most of those remaining were either too old for the task of mining, or they were the wives and children who were left behind to wait.

The one bright and shining thing in her new life as a woman in waiting was her son Jesse. He was now nearly 4 years old, and every day it seemed as though his vocabulary was increasing tenfold. The young Jesse was learning new things every day from those who were included in his circle of life. Of course, the Skyler's were instrumental in his learning, and his mother was extremely important to his growth, but the surprising element in his life was Amos Sutter.

Every day, Jesse would walk with the old man, listening to whatever Amos had to say. Sara knew that the former slave did not have schooling or any formal education, but she recognized that life has a way of teaching people a lot of information that is much more important than what they would learn in some classroom.

In fact, Amos and Jesse were inseparable. As the spring gave way to summer, the two 'partners,' as Sara liked to refer to Amos and Jesse, could be seen walking through to town and out to the small stream to do some "fishin'", as Jesse would mimic the words of his newly discovered friend.

Betty Skylers approached Sara one day, somewhat concerned about something. Without much fanfare, Betty voiced her concerns, "Sara, I'm not the boy's grandmother or anything at all, but I'm somewhat bothered by his being with Mr. Sutter so much."

"Bothered?" Sara answered in surprise.

"Sara, I'm just a bit worried about the two of them being together so much. You know, his being colored and all."

"What?" Sara interjected.

"You know what I mean don't you, Sara? I'm just hearing what other people are saying, Sara. I just don't want Jesse to be hurt by what the other folks are saying, that's all."

Sara knew exactly what the other people in town were saying. She was good and tired about what everyone else was saying.

She spoke out now as if she had heard enough about what other people thought.

"Mrs. Skylers, you know that I have nothin' but respect for what you say, but I think that other people should just keep what they think to theyselves. What they believe or think 'bout Jesse hangin' 'round Amos Sutter is none of their concern."

"Oh, I know, dear. I just hate to see Jesse get hurt, that's all."

"This here is what I have to say 'bout all this, Mrs. Skyler. My Jesse has got himself a grandpa he never had before. He can hang out with Amos all he wants to and no one else has the right to say otherwise."

And with that Sara closed the discussion about who her son could or could not spend his time with.

But Sara knew that if Jesse was going to build a relationship with Amos Sutter, it would be important for the man to understand who Jesse was and how he came to be with her. She decided to have a talk with Amos Sutter as soon as she could.

It wasn't more than two days later that Sara was able to have that discussion with Amos. She guessed that the fishin' wasn't too good as she saw the two of them coming back empty handed. As they walked up to the bungalow, Sara told Jesse to wash up and to play with his toys while she talked with Mr. Sutter.

"Amos," she started after the boy was gone, "they's somethin' I need to let you know 'bout Jesse."

"I knows you been havin' somethin' on yo mind missus."

"Well, I need to let you know 'bout his past and all."

"Go on, ma'am."

This encouragement was all Sara needed to disclose everything about Jesse's real mother and father. She explained to Amos that the boy's real name was not Horne, but that it was Polchev, and that she had unofficially adopted him, using her unmarried name Harlin instead of his birth parents' name. Every bit of Jesse's past was reported to Amos, and he sat intently listening to all she had to say.

Sara even revealed to Amos the plans that Sam and she had made. She told the old gentleman how the dream was to earn enough money in these hills of the Alaskan Territory so that the Horne family could purchase a farm in Central California – preferably in the San Juaquin Valley. She left nothing out, as she told Amos the goals and desires that she and Sam harbored as a couple.

"Well, ma'am, I knows that what you did was bes' for the boy. You's a kindly woman Miss Sara, and the good Lord done use you to raise that little one the proper way. Nuthin' you done told me goes any further to anyone who has no right to know. That's all I gots to say on the matter."

Chapter Seventeen

The summer was fully upon the trio of would-be gold miners, and to date, after three months of searching, digging, and exploring the area a few miles to the east of Fort Yukon, they had not discovered much more than two or three ounces of small gold nuggets that were embedded in a streambed. They had spent an exorbitant amount of time searching these small runoffs and tributaries, but to date there was not much else to show except for some calloused hands and blistered feet.

It was now mid-August, and the three men decided it might be best to move in a more southern direction towards the several small lakes that were in the region just to the east of Jenny Island. This island was located very close to Sixmile Lake and some other lakes around there such as Emile and Otto Lakes. Oddly enough, Sixmile Lake had been given that name because it was barely six miles from Fort Yukon.

The two con-men – Jake and Harry – both thought and said that maybe they would get lucky. Sam was a little more hesitant to call it luck as he no longer believed in such a thing as luck. The only thing he could say was, "Yes, maybe we will be blessed and find what we're looking for there."

So, south they trudged, urging their pack mules to move on, and following close by them with their burdens they carried on their own backs.

It was nearly mid-morning on that warm August day when Sam, Harry, and Jake suddenly eased over a slight rise in the trail only to suddenly come upon a huge, female Kodiak bear with her cub, browsing through the shrub. Simultaneously, the three men knew that they were in a world of hurt. The mother bear released a violent roar and began running toward the three men. As quickly as the bear acted in this way, the men retreated, trying to find sanctuary in the more densely forested area. The pack mules headed off in a totally different direction, but the mother bear was not interested in them. She believed the men to be the greater threat to her cub and pursued them.

Staying as close to one another as they could, the three partners stumbled through the heavily forested, rockier, and hillier region of the woods. The bear was closer to them than they were comfortable having her, and soon it became a race to be able to outrun each other. They knew that keeping ahead of the others meant the bear had a better target to attack.

Jake was by far the fastest of the three, but he was barely able to maintain his lead on the others. They were close on his heels when suddenly it seemed as if the ground disappeared beneath the three men's feet. They were swallowed up, it seemed, by the earth.

Once again, providence reached out with a hand of protection to bless the men with not only salvation from the pursuing bear, but also to grant them the precious gold that they had been seeking. It seemed that they had not just fallen into a hole where the side of a hill met the ground, but they had fallen into a moderately large cavern which contained a long vein of gold-colored metallic rock.

Jake, Harry, and Sam sat in stunned silence. An instant ago they were in a race to save their lives, but now they sat face to face with a deposit of what looked like a major vein of gold. This had to be the 'mother-lode', Harry was thinking as he enraptured by the sight before him. "I believe I have two partners too many," he thought to himself.

After a few minutes of silence, the three men began to stir. They each slowly rose from their seated positions and began to collect their thoughts and senses.

"Gents," Jake was the first to speak. "Are you seein' what I'm seein'?"

"Thank God Almighty!" was all that Sam could utter.

"Yeah," responded Jake, sarcastically. "Thank God and thank that thousand-pound mama bear!"

"What do we do now?" Harry chimed in.

Sam answered by saying, "I believe the next step is in protecting our find. We gotta' get back to Fort Yukon, stake this here claim, and register it as rightly ours."

"Shouldn't one of us stay here to protect it now. You know the saying, 'possession is nine-tenths of the law'" Harry replied.

Jake chimed in, "Yeah, we probably need to have only one of us go in to do that. Maybe whoever goes in to do that should take a bit of this here gold and have it assayed for its value; you know see if its real and all?"

"Your right, Jake," Sam replied.

Harry had his sights on eliminating all his competition to the wealth that was going to be gained here. He spoke up as innocently as he could sound, "Look, you both are absolutely right. While one of us goes to do all that, the other two should find those mules. They do have nearly all our gear you know. Then once that's done, there is no use in letting good time go to waste. Whoever stays can get started mining this here gold."

"But who should go to the assayer's office, Harry?" asked his partner in crime, Jake.

Harry was one shrewd operator and even knew how to con a conman. He answered without hesitation, "It's simple. We know that whoever goes to stake the claim will not run off with the sample – not with all this gold that's still here. So, whoever goes is not gonna' run off."

"I guess he's right, Jake" Sam answered in a trusting manner. "Let's just let him go deal with the paperwork. We can get started and dig up as much of this gold before we have to blast out the rest."

So, as Harry retrieved a small sample of the metal, and gathered up enough supplies to get back to Fort Yukon, Sam and Jake busied themselves with tracking down the mules and setting up a mining site.

With each passing day now in the opening days of September, Sara was getting more and more anxious. It had been about five months now since her Sam and the other two men had left and she was beginning to grow concerned about their well-being. Absence truly does make the heart grow fonder, but it also makes the soul more concerned for the welfare of loved ones. She wanted her husband back home and was thinking that this might not be a very kind winter. Each day that the calendar moved towards the start of the autumn and winter freezes just added to her already high level of anxiety.

It was on a day, when these thoughts were adding to her growing concerns about the safety of Sam, that Harry Brindle came back into the settlement. He was determined to finish what he had set out to do so many months ago when he first tied up with that foolish Jake Ashton. With his sample of the rock that the three men removed from the cave out to the southeast of Fort Yukon, Harry made his way to the assayer's office, located just next to the bank which the miners used to receive payouts for mining discoveries. He wanted to have the rock tested, and to register the claim. In a few days, he would be using the bank next door.

The clerk working at the desk in the office of claims registrations looked up from his work as the tiny bell attached to the top of the entry door jingled. This signified that someone had entered and would be needing assistance. In this case, the person who came into the office was a bedraggled character who looked like he had seen better days. From the smell of the man, it also was apparent that it had been a very long time since he had even touched a bar of soap, let alone bathed.

Putting aside the foul odor emanating from the man, the clerk proceeded to the service desk and asked, "how may I be of assistance, sir?"

Pulling out his small bag containing the metallic rock, Harry said, "I'd like to have this assayed for its worth, and if there is anything of value in it, I wish to register a claim for a mine."

"I can run a little test here to see what you have here. Let me get some things ready, and in the meantime, you can fill out a little bit of paperwork for the claim." the assayer said as he pulled a kit called a blowpipe kit out from under the counter.

The clerk began doing some odd things with the sample that Harry had brought into the office. First, the man chipped off a small piece of the sample and weighed it with a scale. After weighing the piece, he combined some small pellets with it in a clay dish and began heating the combination with a lamp. Then, the man grabbed an L-shaped brass tube with a white piece on the end, set the brass portion near the lamp flame and began to blow gently into the mouthpiece. The flame became noticeably more intense, and it changed from a reddish yellow to a shade of violet.

Several times the clerk would remove tiny glasslike particles from the dish along with some other substances found in the burnt sample, weigh them, and then do so calculations on a piece of paper.

After what seemed an eternity, the clerk looked up at Harry and said, "I'd say it'd be a good idea for you to finish filling out that paperwork. You have quite a find here and you need to stake your claim. I won't bore you with percentages and things like that, but Mister, you've got some high-grade gold ore here."

Harry was about as excited as he had ever been in his life. He was going to be a wealthy man, and those two fools out at the lake will help make sure that was going to take place. At the line which listed the name(s) of the claim registrants, Harry inserted a single name – Harry Brindle. The names of Jake Ashton and Sam Horne were conspicuously missing.

The first step in this most important con of Harry Brindle was completed. Now, the hard part stood before him. All parties involved – other than himself – had to be eliminated. That might take a little bit more thinking and planning, but at least the course had been set. Harry Brindle was one wealthy man!

"It was now a done deal," Harry was thinking as he made his way to the bungalow occupied by Sara Horne and her young son. He didn't know what she was going to do with the boy, but somehow, he had to get her to go out to the claim. The three of them had to be dealt with, and then he would simply disappear before anyone was the wiser. He had to plan this just right so that he would be sure to get away with a tidy sum of gold to be cashed in somewhere far from this place. He was not going to be too greedy, but he was surely going to never have to run another scam again in his entire life.

"Sara! Sara!" Harry yelled as he approached her home.

"Harry?" She responded as she opened the front door and saw the bedraggled partner of her husband standing there at the door. "Harry, what's wrong? Is Sam in hurt?"

"No! Nothing like that. Completely the opposite!"

"Well? What is it, Harry?"

"Ma'am, you are looking at one-third of one of the richest partnerships in all of Alaska!" he exclaimed with really knowing how much gold they had discovered.

Harry went on to explain how they had discovered the cave by narrowly escaping the mother bear; that the claim was now registered, of course leaving out the part about the other three being left off the claim's registry; and that she was needed at the site to help with the mining.

"Sam wants me to just drop everything here and come out, the good Lord knows where to, and help the three of you mine? What about Jesse? What does Sam suppose I will do with him?" were Sara's valid questions.

Lying, Harry responded, "All I know is that Sam is all excited about this here find, and he wants you out there helping us."

"Well, I suppose that the Skyler's will be more than happy to watch Jesse for a while. But Harry, this might take a while to accomplish. You know, I can't just drop the boy off with, ..."

The thought was soon growing in her mind that it might be better to let Amos watch Jesse. She knew that he loved the boy dearly and would not let anything happen to him.

"When are you wanting to leave for the claim, Harry?" she asked as she started gathering up some things for Jesse.

"The sooner the better, ma'am."

"Well, okay. I just need to get some things together. Of course, this does depend on whether or not I can find a suitable place to leave Jesse."

"Oh sure, I understand. Is there anything I can do to help you get the boy ready?"

Plans were made in a relatively short amount of time. Sara gathered up some toys and other items that she knew Amos would need in order to take good care of her son. Then she and Harry, along with Jesse, went to the small room in the back of the store where the Skyler's were allowing Amos to stay. If it was okay with both the Skyler's and Amos, Harry and Sara would be on their way back to the mining claim before the day was over. They could travel the six miles to the site and be there long before the sun began to set.

With Harry carrying some of the things that Sara wanted to take to the mining claim, the two of them were able to cover the six miles in a relatively short amount of time. They arrived at the site around 8:00 at night, but because the sun would not set for another three hours or so, there would be plenty of daylight left to set up her things.

Sam was completely caught off guard when he first saw Harry strolling into the clearing, escorted by his young wife. To say that he was surprised would be an understatement. He was both shocked to see her and angry at Harry for exposing Sara to possible danger by bringing her out here. The more he thought about it the angrier he became and before long, with hands clenched in fists, he approached Harry, ready to talk with his fists if necessary.

Sara could see the old Sam beginning to emerge as she quickly intercepted him on his course of confrontation with Harry. "Sam," she yelled out trying desperately to distract her husband.

Fortunately for Harry, it worked.

"Sam, Sam, it's okay!" Sara said, as she now realized that Harry had lied to her about what Sam wanted. She didn't quite know why Harry had done this, but maybe it was for the best. She began talking with Sam, trying to ease his concerns and anger.

"Sam, you just listen to me. Maybe Harry was wrong for bringing me out here, but it's not like we are all that far from home. It only took us a couple of hours to walk here, and it would take me no time at all to get home if I needed to."

"But Sara, the bear ..."

"Sam, Harry told me all about that. I ain't worried about no bear, Sam."

"Listen Sam," Harry interjected, "I just wanted to share the news with Sara about our find, that's all. I thought that maybe she could help us some, that's all. Oh, by the way, if anyone is interested, we have hit paydirt here. The gold is here and the man at the assayer's office says its good. We're gonna' be rich, Sam!"

Suddenly, the tension in the air began to ease. Sam was visibly calming down, and Sara began to be a little more at ease, knowing that her husband would not beat his partner to death. Now the conversation turned to how they were going to get all this gold out of the hole.

Chapter Eighteen

"So, Harry," Jake began a private conversation when the two con men were alone, "are we suddenly turning honest or something? We been workin' this mine for a couple of weeks, and it seems to me as if we're honest laborers now."

It did seem that their life of crime had been replaced by hard daily labor. Now, it seemed that they had turned into honest men trying to become engaged in gainful employment. They had been digging, shoring up the cave with anything that would serve as timber, and using small charges of dynamite to excavate deeper into the hillside. They had created a mine some thirty feet deep.

"Relax Jake," Harry replied. "I haven't forgotten what we're doing here. It just needs to look like we're serious gold miners, that's all."

"So, have you thought about how we're gonna' get this gold from the other two?" Jake asked.

"Yeah, as a matter of fact, I have been thinking about nothing but that."

"What have you come up with, Harry?"

Harry knew that this was the crucial part of his scheme. He had to coax Jake into doing something that was beyond what he was willing or capable of doing – to murder someone else, or in this case some others. He knew that Jake would be dead set against doing anything like that, but he also knew that this would result in

Jake just being dead. Having already planted a few sticks of dynamite within the cave, he could create a commotion that would lure those two Bible thumpers into the cave. With Jake and the Horne's inside the cave, and the perfect timing, he would be able to ignite the explosives, killing Sam and Sara, and covering up the bodies of all three at the same time.

But Harry knew that the key to the whole ordeal was getting Jake so angry that he would actually want to fight him. So, with a gun perfectly concealed within his jacket, Harry approached Jake and said, "You need to come to the mine with me, Jake. I want to show you something."

Dutifully, Jake tossed away the half-eaten apple he had been consuming and followed Harry as he walked to the cave. Both Sara and Sam were back at the camp, and Harry thought that he saw the two of them actually praying together. A couple of fools, he thought, as he steeled himself for the task ahead of him.

"Listen Jake," Harry started as they were near the mouth of the mine. "Here's what we're gonna' do. I have a couple of sticks of dynamite in set in the mine and they are already set to the charger. We need to get Sara and Sam into this mine alone, and then we can bring the house down on them. They'll be buried in this hill, and we can take what we've mined and get away. There must be at least $70,000 or more in the small amount we've gotten out. We'll divide it two ways and be set for the rest of our lives."

"What are you talkin' 'bout, Harry? Are we murderers now? I ain't doin' that, no way!"

"Listen Jake, you got to. You're in too deep. I want out of this wilderness, and I want out soon, Jake. You are in with me or else!"

"Or else what, Harry?"

"Or else this!" Harry responded pulling out the pistol that he had concealed.

"You're a crazy man, Harry." Jake exclaimed as he tried to move the other man away in order to exit the mine.

He was not going to let Jake leave, not with all that had transpired in the last few minutes. He firmly grasped the man by his arm and pulled him back into the mine forcefully. Jake stumbled and fell as a result of Harry's action. He got up to once again try to leave. That's when Harry pulled the trigger, shooting Jake in the back of the head, killing him instantly.

The sound of the shot echoed through the forest as Sara and Sam were ending their prayers for a blessed day. They looked at each other with alarm. The only thing that sounded like a gunshot was just that – a gunshot! With neither one of them hesitating, they both rushed toward the mine entrance where they thought the sound was coming from.

As soon as Harry had killed Jake, he ran out of the mine and stood waiting next to the device that would ignite the dynamite within the mine. Once he detonated the charges, he would check to make sure that the entrance had collapsed. Then he would grab what precious metal he could and make a hasty retreat out of these woods. He would sell the ore they had taken, close out the claim, and sail away on the boats that were taking passengers back to Fort St. Michael.

Soon, Sam appeared with Sara following close behind him. Looking around to see if there was anything amiss, they both began to call out the names of their partners – Harry and Jake. With no one answering their calls, both of them entered the entrance of the mine. Waiting just a few minutes to give them enough time to move further into the mine shaft, Harry then pushed down on the plunger that would ignite the charges within the hillside mine. Without too much hesitation, a resounding explosion issued forth from the mine.

It had been done. Harry strolled toward what had been the entrance and found only the aftermath of the destruction he had brought upon the orifice of what used to be the mine cave entrance.

The dirt was still settling from the explosion as Harry walked slowly and resolutely back to where they had stacked the bags of mineral ore that the three of them had mined out of the hillside. Loading the sacks onto the two mules who were a bit startled by the recent chaos of the explosion, Harry began leading them away toward Fort Yukon. His work was done!

Chapter Nineteen

It was beginning to be a little bit worrisome for Amos Sutter and the Skyler's. Sara had now been gone for nearly month now, and there was no word from any of the four about what was happening at their claim.

What worried Amos more, and continued to add to his concern was the fact that one morning, as he passed by the port where the steamboats unloaded and took on passengers, he could almost be certain that he saw a fellow who looked an awful lot like one of the two men who partnered up with Sam. Now, as each day passed, Amos's concern turned into downright anxiety.

As the month of September was coming to an end, Amos decided, on a whim, that may the assayer's office might be able to give him some useful information about where the mine was located. What he learned made his blood run cold. The clerk informed him that yes, the mine had produced some gold, and that the registrant on the claim had already sold a quantity to the assayer's office – about $40,000 to be exact. The man, named Harry Brindle had closed his claim on the mine telling the clerk that the mine was 'played out.'

It would take some doing, and a lot of prayer, but he had to get to the mine site to find out what had happened to Sara. He thought that he might need to take some sort of wagon with him, just in case.

The Skyler's were completely in agreement with Amos and were able to secure a team of horses and a wagon that could be maneuvered into the area where Sixmile Lake was located. So, in late September, Amos set out to where he knew the area around the lake in which the mine was located.

Onboard the vessel steaming from Ft. St. Michael to San Francisco, Harry Brindle could be seen within his stateroom smiling with an evil and lascivious grin at the stacks of currency lying on the bed.

Although it had not been the amount of money that he thought it might have been, it was still more than he had ever seen at one time. Counting it for a third or fourth time – he forgot how many times he had counted it – he arrived at the same amount. There on the bed before him was $40,000.

Musing aloud he said, "Harry, you worked hard for all of this. You are now set for some time. You are going to live the high life for once in your life!"

He heard about how people were beginning to settle in Oklahoma Territory. That might be as good a place to go now as anywhere else. He decided to check out all about getting from San Francisco to the Oklahoma Territory. When he eventually ran out of all this money, he was sure there would be easy targets to run his scams against there. Besides, it would be good to be somewhere warm for a change.

Amos Sutter drove the wagon slowly into Fort Yukon. On the back end, he had placed the bodies of the three people whom he had dug and pulled out of the collapsed mine. It seemed that only the opening had been closed, and not too deeply into the mine at that. Nevertheless, after clearing away the ruble, Amos found the gruesome remains of three people. One of them had been shot in the back of the head. It was definitely Jake Ashton. His death must have been from the gunshot wound.

Sadly, the other two were his dear friends, Sara and Sam Horne. From what he could see, they had died from the wounds they received as some of the mine had collapsed on them. It seemed that Sam had pulled himself out of the debris and had dragged himself to the body of Sara. His arms were lying on her as if he were trying to protect her.

With tears streaming down his face, Amos loaded the bodies of his two friends onto the wagon next to the body of Jake Ashton.

The first thing that Amos Sutter did after the funerals of both Sara and Sam Horne was to reregister the claim that Harry Brindle had surrendered. He did not know if any gold could still be mined out of it, but it might be worth a try next year. There was a bit of trouble with Amos registering this claim. The same clerk at the assayer's office who dealt with Harry told him that normally, the waiting for claim registrations for a man of his color would take a few months at least.

What the clerk did not reckon on was having to deal with the weight of the local law enforcement officer and the commander of the army base at Fort Yukon. Both had become Christians since moving to the small but growing community there. They had grown to love Amos as a fellow parishioner and were quite intent on making sure that he was not cheated by anyone just because of the color of his skin. It was a simple matter of the clerk seeing the badge on the sheriff's chest and the gold cluster on the shoulder bars of the commander to convince him to adhere to the rules.

So, the claim was transferred rather than canceled and Amos Sutter became the owner of a mining claim that could possibly be something through which Jesse Harlin could profit.

Another issue related somewhat to the claim on the mine was beginning to arise. This issue was brought up by Jonah and Betty Skyler, and it dealt with a sensitive and compelling problem.

One night, during the deepening winter months, Jonah brings the problem up with Amos. "You know, Amos, we feel like you are just about as close to being a member of our family as if you were born into it."

"Yes sir, I knows that well."

"Well, I think we should talk about what's going to happen to Jesse since his parents are now no longer with us."

"I reckon I'm not followin' you Mr. Skyler."

"Come now, Amos," Jonah sighed. "You must know the trouble you're asking for, raising that boy by yourself."

"We's doin' quite fine, Mr. Skyler."

"Amos," Betty Skyler joined in, "do you remember what you went through when you were getting the claim to the mine settled?"

"Yes'em, I remember."

"Well Amos, that was just for a piece of dirt. With Jesse we're talking about a living boy. A living … Caucasian … boy, Amos."

"Mr. and Mrs Skyler, I respect ya'll in every way. I know that they's real bad people out there. I know that they's people who won't hanker with my being a Negro man and raisin' a white boy. The fact is, they's Negro folks that'll have the same reservations 'bout as all t'other folks."

"What do you mean, Amos," asked Jonah.

"What I means is that peoples is bad no matter what shade o' brown they is. They's bad and mean Caucasians, bad and mean Negros, bad and mean Asians. The book we live by – the Bible? – well, it done tol' us that the heart is wicked, no matter what."

"We know Amos, and you are absolutely right," Betty said, "but we don't want to see you getting hurt in any way. We can protect you here, but you may not be here all that much longer. What will happen when you take Jesse somewhere else. Maybe we should keep him here to make sure he is okay."

"No ma'am. Sara wanted me to take care o' the boy for her should anythin' happen to her or Sam. He stays with me, and we will depend on the Lord for his provision,"

Amos knew deep down inside that the Skyler's were really just looking for someone to take care of their store in the future. He was determined to keep charge of Jesse, work the mine, and save what he could from what he could pull out of it for the boy's future. Jesse was his charge, and he would die defending the child and ensure that his mother's wishes were carried out. Sara had sacrificed her life for not just her son, but also for her faith in Jesus Christ. He knew that she was a blessed woman, and that she touched the lives of all with whom she came into contact. If one young, seemingly defenseless woman could give her life for her faith and her family, then he would do the same with every ounce of strength he had. Jesse was her legacy, and that legacy was worth saving.

About the Author

Larry Trapp was born and raised in the southern San Juaquin Valley of California in the city of Bakersfield. Larry likes to remind people who have never been to California or don't know much about it that it is an extremely complex state demographically. It is probably one of the most ultra-liberal states in America, but there are vast areas of land containing large numbers of the population who hold very traditional beliefs about God, family, and the nation. Larry was raised and still lives in a region of the state that holds politically conservative ideologies, and this has had a huge impact on his worldview and a deep faith in God.

After graduating from Bakersfield High School (go "Drillers"!), Larry went to Riverside to attend what was then known as California Baptist College (now called California Baptist University). He majored in music there but had to return home to care for his disabled mother. By 1968, to avoid being drafted into the infantry, Larry enlisted in the Army and eventually was trained to be an air traffic control radar operator. After serving in Vietnam for 1½ years, and being honorably discharged in 1971, Larry returned to college, attending Bakersfield Community College. Larry likes to tell most people that he successfully crammed four years of college into twenty-eight years, and finally, in 1999, earned his Bachelor of Arts degree in Organizational Management. During those 28 years of instruction, Larry was able to attend and pass many different types of courses including a lot of studies of American History and Western Civilization. College also afforded him the ability to conduct research on many different subjects.

While teaching the Logic and Rhetoric phases (7th to 12th grades) at Heritage Oak School in Tehachapi, California, Larry was given and took the opportunity to earn his master's degree in education. Heritage Oak School uses a Classical/Christian pedagogical approach to instruction. The key guide to this type of learning is taken from the book by Dorothy Sayers titled The Lost Tools of Learning. Sadly, in March 2020, all the schools in California were forced to adhere to the restrictions of online instruction. This was the indicator for Larry that it was now time to retire from actively teaching in the classroom, and in June 2020, Larry officially retired from work, and then set out writing the book you are holding that had been in the planning stages for nearly ten years.

Larry has been married to his lovely and loving wife Merryl for nearly 46 years (since December 10, 1976). He has two sons, Wayne who is 40 years old, and David who is 37. He is also the proud grandfather of Brogan (14 years old) and Rorie (9 years old).

The author also wants to testify of his deep abiding faith in the Lord Jesus Christ. He has been born again since February 1973 and has known and experienced a wide range of emotions in serving the Lord. It is also abundantly clear to Larry that following the Lord is not for the weak of heart. There are adventures in serving God which goes far beyond any that one can find on their own. Following the leadership of God will not insure a pain-free life. Quite the opposite. But it does ensure that you have someone with you whenever those heartaches and challenges come your way.

God Bless!

CPSIA information can be obtained
at www.ICGtesting.com
Printed in the USA
LVHW111433081022
730256LV00021B/175